Fleet Captain Nils Kivi took one look at his instruments and read death . . . Vibrations of impact and shearing still toned in the metal around him. Weightlessness, as the ion blast died, was like being pitched off a cliff. He heard a wail as air escaped, then a clash as the pierced section was automatically closed off. None of it registered. His entire self was speared on the needle of the radiation meter . . . *'Abandon ship!'*

Also by Poul Anderson in Panther Science Fiction

Poul Anderson

Orbit Unlimited

Panther

Granada Publishing Limited
Published in 1976 by Panther Books Ltd
Frogmore, St Albans, Herts AL2 2NF

First published in Great Britain by
Sidgwick & Jackson Ltd 1974
Copyright © by Almat Publishing Corporation 1961
Acknowledgments: Portions of this book appeared,
in somewhat different form, in *Astounding Science
Fiction* for January 1959 and January 1960, and in
Fantastic Universe for October 1959
Made and printed in Great Britain by
Richard Clay (The Chaucer Press) Ltd
Bungay, Suffolk
Set in Linotype Times

Part 1 : Robin Hood's Barn

1

Svoboda was about sixty years old. He did not know his exact age. The Lowlevel seldom counted such things, and his earliest memory was of weeping in an alley while rain fell past an overhead beltway that roared. Afterward his mother died and someone who claimed to be his father but probably wasn't sold him to Inky the thiefmaster.

Sixty was ancient for a man of the masses, whether he slunk cat-fashion through soot and noise and sudden death in a city Lowlevel or – more healthfully if with less freedom – squirmed along a mine shaft or tended engine on a plankton reaper. For an upper-level Citizen, or a Guardian, sixty was only middle-aged. Svoboda, who had spent half his life in either category, looked as old as Satan but could hope for another two decades.

If you wanted to call it hope, he thought wryly.

His left foot was paining him again. It was a lump within the special shoe. When he was twelve or so, scrambling over a garden wall with a silver chalice contributed by one Engineer Harkavy, an explosive slug from a guard's pistol had smashed the bones. He got away somehow, but it was a cruel thing to happen to one of the most promising lads in the Brotherhood. Inky reapprenticed him to a fence, which forced him to learn reading and writing and thus started him on a long road up. Twenty-five years afterward, when Svoboda was Commissioner of Astronautics, a medic recommended prosthetizing the broken foot.

'I can make you one that you can hardly tell from the real thing, sir,' he offered.

'Undoubtedly,' said Svoboda. 'I have seen our older Guardians tottering around with prosthetic hearts and prosthetic stomachs and a sort of prosthetic eye. I am sure the onward march of science will soon come to a prosthetic brain, which can hardly be told from the real thing. Some of my colleagues lead me to think this has already been achieved.' He shrugged skinny shoulders. 'No. I'm too busy. Later, perhaps.'

The busyness consisted in breaking out of the Astronautical Department, a notorious dead end into which nervous superiors had maneuvered him. And having done so, he was at once preoccupied with something else. There had never been time. You had to run pretty fast just to stay where you were.

How many people nowadays had read *Alice*? he wondered.

But the foot did often pain him. He stopped to let the throbbing ease.

'Are you all right, sir?' asked Iyeyasu.

Svoboda looked at the giant and smiled. His other six guards were nonentities, the usual efficient impersonal killing machines. Iyeyasu did not pack a gun; he was a karate man, and he could reach into your rib cage and pull your lungs out if you displeased Svoboda.

'I'll do,' said the Commissioner of Psychologics. 'Don't inquire exactly what I'll do, but there must be something.'

Iyeyasu offered an arm and his master leaned on it. The contrast was ridiculous. Svoboda stood barely 150 centimeters tall, with a hairless dome of skull and a face all dark wrinkles and scimitar nose. His childish frame was gaudy in a cloak like fire, iridescent high-collared tunic, and deep-blue trousers cut in the latest bell-bottomed style. Whereas the Okinawan wore gray, and had a shoulder-length black mane and hands deformed by a lifetime's cracking bricks and punching through boards.

Svoboda fumbled with yellow-stained fingers after a cigaret. He stood on a landing terrace, immensely high up. Below was none of the parkscape which most Commissioners chose for their buildings; Svoboda had put his departmental tower in the same city which spawned him. It stretched under his feet as far as he could gaze through

6

airborne filth. But past the floating docks, on the world's eastern edge, he could see a mercury gleam that was the open Atlantic.

Dusk was creeping over the planet. Spires etched themselves black against the surly red remnants of sundown. Highlevel walls and streets began to glow. Lowlevel was a darkness beneath, and a muted unending growl of beltways, generators, autofactories, sparks to show a window waking to life or a pedicar headlamp or the flashbeams of men going in cudgel-armed parties for fear of the Brotherhood.

Svoboda drew smoke through his nostrils. His eyes wandered past the aircar which had borne him here from his oceanic house, to the sky. Venus stood forth, white against royal blue. He sighed and gestured at it. 'Do you know,' he said, 'I'm almost glad the colony there has been discontinued. Not because it wasn't paying for itself, though God would know we can't waste resources these days, if God existed. For a better reason.'

'What is that, sir?' Iyeyasu sensed that the Commissioner wanted to talk. They had been together for many years.

'Now there's one place you can go to get away from humankind.'

'Venus air is no good, sir. You can go to the stars and get away, and not wear armor.'

'But nine years in deepsleep to the nearest star! A bit extreme for a vacation.'

'Yes, sir.'

'And then the planets you find are as bad as Venus ... or they're like Earth, but not *enough* like Earth, and men break their hearts. Come on, let's go play at being important.'

Svoboda leaned back onto his crutch and went quickly over the terrace, through an arched portal and down a long luminous-walled corridor. His guards fanned out, ahead and behind, their eyes never still; Iyeyasu stayed close. Not that Svoboda expected assassins. There was a night shift at work, because Psychologics was a major fief within the

Federation government, but at this hour there would be no underlings on this floor.

At the hall's end was a teleconference room. Svoboda hobbled to an easy chair, Iyeyasu helped him into it and set a desk in front of him. Most of the men who looked from the screens had advisors beside them. Svoboda was alone, except for his guards. He had always worked alone.

Premier Selim nodded. Behind his image was a window opening on palm trees. 'Ah, there you are, Commissioner,' he said. 'We were just beginning to wonder.'

'I apologize for my lateness,' answered Svoboda. 'As you know, I never transact business from my home, so I had to come here for the conference. Well, a caisson under my house sprang a leak, the gyrostabilizers failed, and before I knew what had happened I was reading the time off a seasick octopus. It was ten minutes slow.'

Security Chief Chandra blinked, opened a bearded mouth to protest, then nodded. 'Ah, you make a joke. I see. Ha.' He sat in India at sunrise; but the rulers of Earth were used to irregular hours.

'Let us begin,' said Selim. 'We will dispense with formalities. However, before we start the business at hand, is there anything else of urgency?'

'Er—' Rathjen, the present Commissioner of Astronautics, spoke timidly. He was the weak son of the late Premier; his father had given him this post and nobody since had bothered to take it away. 'Er, yes, gentlemen, I should again like to raise the question of repair funds for ... I mean to say, we have several perfectly good spaceships which only need a few million in repair funds to, er, reach the stars again. And then the astronautical academies. Really, the quality of new recruits is as low as the quantity. I should think, that is, if we – Mr. Svoboda especially, it seems to be in his department – an intensive propaganda campaign, directed at younger sons of the Guardian families ... or Citizens of professional status ... persuading them of the importance, giving the profession the, er, the glamor it once had—'

'Please,' interrupted Selim. 'Another time.'

'I might make a remark, though,' said Svoboda.

'What?' Novikov of Mines turned a surprised eye on him. 'You are the one who brought this special conference about. Do you want to waste it on irrelevancies?'

' "Nothing is irrelevant," ' murmured Svoboda.

'What?' said Chandra.

'I was only quoting Anker, the philosophical father of Constitutionalism,' Svoboda told him. 'Someday you might try understanding the things you want to suppress. I have been assured that it works wonders.'

Chandra flushed with annoyance. 'But I don't want —' he began, and decided otherwise.

Selim looked baffled. Rathjen said plaintively, 'You were going to comment on my business, Mr. Svoboda.'

'So I was.' The small man struck a fresh cigaret and inhaled deeply. His eyes, a startling electric blue in the mummy face, leaped from screen to screen. 'Commissioner Novikov could give you a good reason for the decay of astronautics: more people and fewer resources every day. We can no more afford interstellar exploration than we can afford representative government. The vestiges of both are being eliminated as fast as the anguish of yourself, and the Constitutionalists, permits. Which I know is not as fast as some of you gentlemen would like. But by pushing social change too hard, the government provoked the North American Rebellion twenty years ago.' He grinned. 'Therefore we must take the lesson to heart and not goad the Astronautical Department into revolt. It's easier to operate a few spaceships for a few more decades than to storm barricades of filing cabinets manned by desperate bureaucrats waving the bloody flag in triplicate. But you on your side, Mr. Rathjen, must not expect us to expand, or even maintain, your fleet.'

'Mr. Svoboda!' gasped Rathjen.

Selim cleared his throat. 'We all know the Psychologics Commissioner's sense of humor,' he said ponderously. 'But since he has mentioned the Constitutionalists, I trust he

9

means to proceed to our real business.'

The dozen faces turned upon Svoboda and did not let go. He veiled his own stare in smoke and replied, 'Very well. I daresay Commissioner-baiting is a cruel sport, and instead I should pick good-looking Citizen girls off the streets for several weeks of Special Instruction.' Now Larkin of Pelagiculture was the one who glared. 'Perhaps you aren't all familiar with the issue on hand. I've submitted a new report on the Constitutionalists to Premier Selim, Mr. Chandra, and the Commandant of North America. It proved so controversial that the whole Guardian Commission has been asked to debate it.'

He nodded at Selim. The Premier's harsh gray face looked a bit startled. It was almost as if Svoboda had given him permission to go ahead. He harrumphed, glanced at the paper on his desk, and said:

'The trouble is, the Constitutionalists are not a political group. If they were, we could round them up tomorrow. They are not even formally organized, and there is no total agreement among them. What they subscribe to is only a philosophy.'

'Bad,' murmured Svoboda. 'Philosophies rationalize emotional attitudes. The very name of this one is a Freudian slip.'

'What's that?' asked Novikov.

'You ought to know,' said Svoboda sweetly. 'You're rather an expert. To continue, though. Officially, the name "Constitutionalism" refers merely to an attitude toward the physical universe, an advocacy of bashing thought patterns on the constitution of reality. Anti-mysticism, you might say. But I grew up here in North America, where half the population still speaks English. And I can tell you that in English, that word Constitution is loaded! The North American insurrection was brought on when the Federation government persistently and flagrantly violated – not the spirit of their poor old much-amended Constitution; they were always good at that themselves – but the letter of it.'

'I know that much,' said Chandra. 'Don't think I haven't

investigated these so-called philosophers. I know that many were in the revolt, or had fathers who were. But they aren't dangerous. They may grumble to themselves, but as a class they're not doing so badly. They have no reason to start another futile uprising.' He shrugged. 'Actually, most of them must be intelligent enough to see that that Bill of Rights or whatever it was simply doesn't work when there are half a billion people on their continent, eighty percent illiterate.'

'What are they, anyway?' asked Dilolo of Agriculture.

'Mostly North American,' said Svoboda. 'I mean of the old stock, not the more recent Oriental immigrants. But their doctrines are spreading through educated Citizens of every race, over the whole world. I imagine if you quizzed, you'd find a fourth of the literate population – rather more than that among scientists and technicians – in substantial agreement with Constitutionalist doctrine. Though of course not so many would consciously think of themselves as Constitutionalists.'

'In other words,' said Chandra, 'it's not just another new religion. Not for the yuts. Nor for Guardians – as a rule' – he gave Svoboda a lingering glance – 'or top-level Citizens. I know that already. I've investigated too. And I found Constitutionalism appealed chiefly to the hard-working, prosperous-but-not-rich man: the sober, solid type, who has won a little more status than his father and hopes his son may have a little more than himself. Such people aren't revolutionaries.'

'And yet,' said Svoboda, 'Constitutionalism is becoming a great deal stronger than you would expect from the small number of formal adherents.'

'How?' asked Larkin.

'You leave your engineers' daughters alone, don't you?' said Svoboda.

'What has that – I mean, explain yourself before I lodge a criticism!'

Svoboda grinned. He could break Larkin any time he chose. 'The Guardians have the power,' he said, 'but what's

11

left of Earth's middle class has the influence. There's a distinction. The masses don't try to imitate the Guardians, or really listen to us. The gap is too great. Their natural leaders are the lower-middle-class Citizenry. Who in turn look to the middle and upper middle classes. As for us Guardians, we may decree the irrigation of Morocco, and round up a million convicts to dig canals and die; but only if an upper-middle-class engineer has assured us it's feasible. He probably advised it in the first place!

'The trouble with Constitutionalism is that it's too likely to give this middle class an awareness of their potential power, and thereby start them agitating for a corresponding voice in the government. Which could be more than a little bit lethal to us.'

There was a pause. Svoboda finished his cigaret and struck another. He felt the air wheeze in his throat. All the world's biomedics couldn't make up the abuse he visited on lungs and bronchial tubes. *But what else is there to do?* he thought in his private darkness.

Selim said, 'This is not a question of menace to ourselves personally, gentlemen. But the Psychologics Commissioner has persuaded me that if we care about our children and grandchildren, we must think seriously on this matter.'

'You don't mean arrest the Constitutionalists en masse?' asked Larkin, alarmed. 'But you can't do that! I know how many of my key technical personnel are – I mean, it would be a disaster to every pelagic city on Earth!'

'You see?' smiled Svoboda. He shook his head. 'No, no. Besides such practical, immediate difficulties, large-scale arrests might provoke new conspiracies to overthrow the Federation. I'm not that stupid, my friends. I propose to undermine the Constitutionalist movement, not batter at it.'

'But see here,' objected Chandra, 'if it's a simple question of a propaganda campaign against these beliefs, you don't need the whole Guardian Commission to —'

'More than propaganda. I want to close the Constitutionalist schools. Never mind the adults. Let them go on thinking what they choose. It's the next generation that we're worried about.'

'You wouldn't let their brats into *our* schools, would you?' gasped Dilolo.

'I assure you, they don't have vermin,' said Svoboda. 'Though they might be infected with a little originality. But no, I'm not that drastic. However, my idea is radical enough to need full Commission approval. I want to revive the old system of free compulsory education.'

After the hubbub had faded, which it did because he sat and ignored it, he went on: 'Oh, modified, to be sure. I don't plan to rope in the hopeless 75 percent of the population. Let them go their merry way. We can easily rig admission standards so as to keep them out. What I do want is a decree that all basic education will be financed by the government and must meet official requirements. Which means my requirements. I'll leave the apprentice centers, academies, monasteries, and other useful or harmless educational institutions alone. But the schools maintained according to Constitutionalist principles will be found to have a deplorably low standard. I'll fire their teachers and install some good loyal hacks.'

'There'll be trouble,' warned Dilolo.

'Yes. But not too much. Of course the parents will object. But what can they say? Here the state, in a sudden gush of benevolence, is lifting the burden of school costs off their shoulders (never mind where the taxes come from) and making sure that their children will be properly taught and properly adjusted to society. If they want to instill their funny little beliefs in addition, why, they can do so in the evenings and on holidays.'

'Ha!' Chandra laughed. 'A lot of good that will do.'

'Just so,' agreed Svoboda. 'A philosophy has to be lived. You can't acquire it in an hour a day from a weary father who lectures you while you'd rather be out playing ball. Your non-Constitutionalist classmates are going to ridicule your oddities. And at the same time, the parents will scarcely be able to stir up popular support. This isn't the

13

kind of issue which brings on revolutions. We will, almost literally, kill Constitutionalism in its cradle.'

'You haven't yet proven that it's worth the trouble of killing,' said Novikov.

Larkin put in vindictively: 'I know why it is. Because Mr. Svoboda's only son is a Constitutionalist, that's the reason. Because they broke up over the issue ten years ago and haven't spoken since!'

Svoboda's eyes turned quite pale. He held them on Larkin for a very long time. Larkin began to squirm, twisted a pencil in his fingers, looked away, looked back, and wiped sweat off his face.

Svoboda continued to stare. It grew very still in the room. In all the rooms, around the earth.

At the end, Svoboda sighed. 'I shall lay the detailed facts and analysis before you, gentlemen,' he said. 'I shall prove that Constitutionalism has the seeds of social change in it: radical change. Do you want the Atomic Wars back again? Or even a bourgeoisie strong enough to try for a voice in government? That sounds less dramatic, but I assure you, the Guardians will be killed just as dead. Now in order to prove my contention, I shall begin with—'

2

The address which Theron Wolfe had given turned out to be on the fiftieth floor in a district once proud. Joshua Coffin could remember almost a century back, how this building had reared alone among trees and gardens, and only a dun cloud in the east bespoke the city. But now the city had engulfed it with mean plastic shells of tenement. In another generation, this would be Lowlevel.

'However,' said Wolfe, 'I've lived here my whole life and gotten a sentimental attachment to the place.'

'I beg your pardon?' Coffin was startled.

'It might be hard for a spaceman to realize.' Wolfe smiled. 'Or for most better-to-do Citizens, as far as that goes. They are even more nomadic than you, First Officer. Generally you have to be of Guardian family, with an estate, or one of the nameless mass too poor to move anywhere, to strike roots nowadays. But I am a middle-class exception.' He stroked his beard and added after a moment, sardonically: 'Besides which, it would be hard to find a comparable apartment. You must realize that Earth's population has doubled since you left.'

'I know,' said Coffin, more brusquely than he had intended.

'But come in.' Wolfe took his arm and led him off the terrace. They entered a living room archaic with broad windows, solid furniture, paneling which might be actual wood, shelves of books both folio and micro, a few age-cracked oil paintings. The merchant's wife, plain and fifty-ish, bowed to her guest and went back to the kitchen. She actually cooked her own food? Coffin was irrationally touched.

'Please sit down.' Wolfe waved a hand at a worn, ugly chair. 'An antique, but highly functional. Unless you prefer the modern fashion of sitting cross-legged on a cushion.

Even Guardians are beginning to think it's stylish.' Horse-hair rustled under Coffin's weight. 'Smoke?'

'No, thank you.' The spaceman realized his tone had been too prim and tried to rationalize. 'The habit isn't common in my profession. Mass ratio, you know, approximately nine to one for an interstellar journey —' He stopped. 'Pardon me. I didn't mean to talk shop.'

'Oh, but I would much prefer you did. That's why I invited you here, after catching your lecture.' Wolfe took a cigarillo from the box for himself. 'Drink?'

Coffin accepted a small glass of dry sherry. The genuine article, doubtless fabulously expensive. In a way it was a shame to waste it on his unappreciative palate. But the Lord had spoken plainly about the sin of idle self-indulgence.

He looked at Wolfe. The merchant was big, plump, still hearty in middle age, with a neat gray Van Dyke. The broadness of his face gave him a curious withdrawn look, as if a part of him always stood aside from the world and watched. He wore a formal robe over dress pajamas, but his feet were in slippers. He sat down, sipped, rolled smoke around his mouth, and said, 'A shame so few people heard your lecture, First Officer. It was most interesting.'

'I am not a very good speaker,' said Coffin, correctly.

'The subject matter, though. To think, a planet of Epsilon Eridani where man can live!'

Coffin felt a thickness of anger. Before he could stop himself, his tongue threw out: 'You must be the thousandth person who has said I was at Epsilon Eridani. For your information, that star was visited decades ago, and has no planets of use to any Christian. It is e Eridani which the *Ranger* visited. I thought you heard my lecture.'

'Slip of my mind. Astronautics is so seldom discussed these days. Sorry.' Wolfe was more urbane than contrite.

Coffin bowed his head, hot-cheeked. 'No. I beg your pardon, sir. I was heedless and ill-mannered.'

'Forget it,' said Wolfe. 'I believe I understand why you're so tense. How long were you away, now? Eighty-seven

16

years, of which five, plus watch time in space, were spent awake. It was the climax of your career, an experience such as is granted few men. Then you came back. Your home was gone, your kinfolk scattered, the people and mores changed almost beyond recognition. Worst of all, hardly a soul cares. You offer them a new world – the habitable planet men have dreamed of discovering for two centuries of space exploration – and they yawn at you when they do not jeer.'

Coffin sat quiet a while, twirling the sherry glass in his fingers. He was a long man with a jagged Yankee face under hair just starting to turn gray. He still affected snug-fitting tunic and trousers of black, knife-creased, with gold buttons bearing the American eagle. Even in the space service, such a uniform was ludicrously outdated.

'Well,' he said at last, struggling for words, 'I expected a ... a different world ... when I came back. Naturally. But somehow I did not expect it would be different in this fashion. We, my companions and I, like every interstellar spaceman, we knew we had chosen a special way of life. But it was in the service of man, which is the service of God. We expected to return to the Astronautic Society, at least, our own spacemen's nation within the nations – do you understand that? But the Society was so *dwindled*.'

Wolfe nodded. 'Not many people realize it yet, First Officer,' he said, 'but space travel is dying.'

'Why?' mumbled Coffin. 'What have we done, that this is visited upon us?'

'We have eaten up our resources with the same abandon with which we have increased our numbers. So the Four Horsemen have ridden out on their predictable path. Exploration is becoming too costly.'

'But – substitutes – new alloys, aluminum must still be abundant – thermonuclear energy, thermionic conversion, dielectric storage —'

'Oh, yes.' Wolfe blew a smoke ring. 'Insufficient, though. Theoretically, we can supply unlimited amounts of fusion power. But there's so little for that power to work on. Light metals and plastics can only do so much, then you need

17

steel. Machines need oil. Well, lean ores can be processed, organics can be synthesized, and so forth. But at a steadily rising cost. And what you do produce has to be spread thinner each year: more people. Of course, there's no longer any pretense at equal sharing. If we tried that, everybody would be down on Lowlevel. Instead, the rich get richer and the poor get poorer. The usual historic pattern, Egypt, Babylon, Rome, India, China, now the entire Earth. So the conscientious Guardian (there are more than you might think) doesn't feel right about spending millions, which could be used to alleviate quite a bit of Citizen misery, on mere discovery. And the non-conscientious Guardian doesn't give a damn.'

Coffin was startled. He looked hard at the other.

'I have heard mention of something called, er, Constitutionalism,' he said slowly. 'Do you subscribe to the doctrine?'

'More or less,' admitted Wolfe. 'Though that's a rather gaudy name for a very simple thing, an ideal of seeing the world as it actually is and behaving accordingly. Anker never called his system anything in particular. But Laird was a rather gaudy man, and—' He paused, smoked with the care of a thrifty person remembering what tobacco cost, and resumed: 'You're probably as much of a Constitutionalist, First Officer, as the average among us.'

'I beg your pardon, no. It seems, from what I've heard, to be a pagan – a Gentile belief.'

'But it isn't a belief. That's the whole point. We're among the last holdouts against a rising tide of Faith. The masses, and lately even a few upper-levels, turn via mysticism and marijuana toward a more tolerable pseudo-existence. I prefer to inhabit the objective universe.'

Coffin grimaced. He had seen abominations. There was a smiling idol where the white church in which his father had preached once overlooked the sea.

He changed the subject: 'But don't the leaders, at least, understand that space travel is the only way to escape the economic trap? If Earth's growing exhausted, we have an

18

entire galaxy of planets.'

'That doesn't help Earth much,' said Wolfe. 'Consider the problem of hauling minerals nine years from the nearest star, with a nine-to-one mass ratio. Or how much bottom do you think it would take to drain off population faster than it will be replaced here at home? Though Rustum were paradise – and you admit yourself, it has serious drawbacks from the human point of view – not many thousand people could go there to live.'

'But the tradition would be kept alive,' argued Coffin. 'Even on Earth, the knowledge that there *was* a colony, a place where a man who found life here unendurable could go – wouldn't that be valuable?'

'No,' said Wolfe bluntly. 'The wage slave Citizen – sometimes, on Lowlevel, an actual slave, in spite of fancy doubletalk about contract – he can't afford such an expensive passage. And why should the state pay his fare? It won't lessen the number of mouths at home; it will only make the state that much poorer, in its efforts to fill those mouths. Nor is the Citizen himself interested, as a rule. Do you think an ignorant, superstitious child of crowds and pavements and machines can survive, plowing alien soil on an empty world? Do you think he even wants to try?' He spread his hands. 'As for the literate, technically minded class of people, those who could make a go of the project, why should they? They have it pretty good here.'

'I was becoming aware of this,' nodded Coffin.

Wolfe's wide face drew into a grin. 'Also – imagine this colony were, somehow, established. Would you want to go live there yourself?'

'Good heavens, no!' Coffin jerked upright.

'Why not, since you're so anxious that it be founded?'

'Because ... because I'm a spaceman. My life is interstellar exploration, not farming or mining. There wouldn't be any spaceships operating out of Rustum for generations. The colonists will have too much else to do. I think such a colony would benefit mankind as a whole; from a selfish angle, I was hoping it would revive interest in space travel.

But it's not my line of work.'

'Exactly. And I am a dealer in fabrics. And my neighbor Israel Stein thinks exploration is a glorious enterprise, but he himself teaches music. My friend John O'Malley is a protein chemist, who would certainly be useful as such on a new planet, and he goes skindiving and once he blew several years' savings on a hunting trip; but his wife has ambitions for their children. And there are others who love their comfort, such as it is; or are afraid; or feel too deeply rooted; or name your own reason. All interested, all sympathetic to your idea, but let someone else do the work. The tiny handful of people you might get who are ready, willing, and able to go, are too few to finance the trip. Q.E.D.'

'So it seems.' Coffin stared into his empty glass.

'But I've seen this much for myself,' he said after a while, his words wrenched and slow. 'I've been forced to realize my profession is on the way out. And it's the only profession open to me. More important, the only one suitable for my children, if I ever have any. For I'd have to marry within the Society. I couldn't find a decent home life anywhere else —' He stopped.

'I know,' gibed Wolfe, not very sharply. 'You beg my pardon. Never mind. Times change, and you are from out of time. I shall not dwell upon the fact that my oldest daughter is a Guardian's mistress, nor raise your hair by remarking that this doesn't trouble me in the least. Because there are some rather more significant changes on Earth in recent months, of which I do disapprove, and they are the main reason I invited you here tonight.'

Coffin looked up. 'What?'

Wolfe cocked his head. 'I believe dinner is about ready. Come, First Officer.' He took his guest's arm again. 'Your lecture was admirably dry and factual, but I'd like a still more detailed description. What Rustum is like, what equipment would be needed to establish a colony of what minimum size, cost estimates ... everything. I assume you would rather talk that kind of shop than make polite noises at me. Well, here's your chance!'

3

Even among his admirers, there were many who would have been astonished to learn that Torvald Anker was still alive. They knew he was born a century ago and that he had never been rich enough to afford elaborate medical care; for he would give a pauper boy with intelligence the right to sit at his feet and question him that he refused a wealthy young dullard who offered good fees. So it seemed natural that he would have died.

His writings bore out that impression. The magnum opus, which men were yet debating, was now sixty years old. The last book, a small volume of essays, was published twenty years back, and had been another gentle anachronism, the style as easy and the thought as careful as if Earth still held a country or two where speech was free. Since then he had lived in his tiny house on the Sognefjord, avoiding the publicity which he had never courted. The district was a fragment of an older world, where a sparse population lived largely by individual effort, men spoke with deliberateness in a beautiful language and cared that their children be educated. Anker taught elementary school for a few hours a day, received food and housekeeping in return, and divided the rest of his time between a garden and a final book.

On a morning in early summer, when dew had not quite left his roses, he entered the cottage. It was centuries old, with a red tile roof above ivied walls. From here a man could look down hundreds of meters, wind, sun, and stone, a patch of wildflowers, a single tree, until he saw cliff and cloud reflected in the fjord. Sometimes a gull sailed past the study window.

Anker sat down at his desk. For a moment he rested, chin in hand. The climb had been long, up from the water's edge, and he had often been forced to stop for breath. His

21

tall thin body had grown so frail he thought he could feel the sunshine streaming through. But it needed little sleep, and when the light nights came – *the sky was like white roses*, someone had written – he must go down to the fjord.

Well. He sighed, brushed an unruly lock off his forehead, and swiveled the 'writer into position. The letter from young Hirayama was first on the correspondence pile. It was not very well written, but it had been written, with an immense desire to say, and that was what counted. Anker was not opposed to the visiphone as such, but quite apart from avoiding interruptions of thought, he had a duty not to own one. The young men must be forced to write if they wanted contact with him, because writing was as essential to the discipline of the mind as conversation, perhaps more so, and elsewhere it was a vanishing skill.

His fingers tapped the keys.

'My dear Saburo,

'Thank you for your confidence in me. I fear it is misplaced. What reputation I have has been gained largely by imitating Socrates. The longer I think upon matters, the more I believe that the touchstone is the epistemological question. How do we know what we know, and what is it we know? From this query a degree of enlightenment occasionally comes. Though I am not at all sure that enlightenment is very similar to wisdom.

'However, I shall try to give definite answers to the problems you bring me, keeping always in mind that the only real answers are those a person finds for himself. But remember that these are the opinions of one who has long shut himself away from modern reality. I think this has afforded a gain in perspective, but I look out of an old reality, now becoming quite alien, out of salt water and rowan trees and huge winter nights, on the active human world. Surely you are far more competent to handle its practical details than I.

'First, then, I do not recommend that you devote your life to philosophy, or to basic scientific research. "The time is out of joint," and there would be nothing for you but a

22

sterile repetition of what other men have said and done. In this judgment I am guided by no Spenglerian mystique of an aged civilization, but by the very hard-headed observation of Donne that no man is an island. Be you never so gifted, you cannot work alone; the cross-fertilization of equally interested colleagues, the whole atmosphere, must be there, or originality becomes impossible. Doubtless the biological potential of a Periclean era or a Renaissance always exists: genetic statistics guarantees that. But social conditions must then determine the extent to which this potential is realized, and even the major forms of expression it takes. I hope I am not being a sour old man in thinking that the present age is as universally barren as the Rome of Commodus. These things happen.

'But – second – you ask implicitly if something can be done to change this. In all frankness, I have never believed so. There may be theoretical ways, as it is theoretically possible to turn winter into summer by hastening the planet along its orbit. But practical limitations intervene. And it is just as well that mortal men with mortal vision do not have the power of destiny.

'You seem to think that I was, on the contrary, once active in politics, a founder of the Constitutionalist movement. This is a popular fallacy. I had nothing to do with it, and never even met Laird. (He is rather a mysterious figure anyway, I gather, suddenly appearing without any background – presumably of Lowlevel birth, self-educated – and vanishing as completely after a decade. Murdered, perhaps?) He was an enthusiastic and understanding reader of mine, but made no attempt at personal contact. He said he was only applying my principles to a concrete situation. His phenomenal rise came after the suppression of the North American revolt and the abolition of the last pretense at a sovereign American government. A crushed, despairing socio-economic-ethnic group turned toward a leader who put their inchoate beliefs into sharp focus and offered them a practical set of rules to live by. Actually these rules

23

amounted to little more than the traditional virtues of patience, courage, thrift, industry, with an interwoven scientific rationalism, but if it has heartened them in their comeback I am honored that Laird quoted me.

'However, I see no long-range hope for them. The tide is ebbing too strongly. And now, I hear, the masters have decided to eliminate Constitutionalism as a danger to the status quo. It is being very cleverly done, in the guise of free education; but it amounts to absorbing the next generation into the general ruck. Let me be grateful that this poor district does not qualify for a public school.

'If we cannot reform society, then, can we save ourselves? There is a way. As the Old Americans would have put it: *Get the hell out!* The monastic orders of the post-Roman past, or of feudal India, China, and Japan, did this, in effect; and I note that their latter-day equivalent is becoming more prominent every decade. It has been my own solution too, though I prefer being an anchorite to a cenobite. The advice grieves me, Saburo, but this may be the only answer for you.

'There was once another way, Christian leaving the City of Destruction in the most literal sense. American history is full of examples, Puritan, Quaker, Catholic, Mormon. And today the stars are a new and more splendid America.

'But I fear this is not the right century for such an escape. The pioneering misfits I speak of departed from a vigorous society which took expansion for granted. It is not characteristic of moribund civilizations to export their radicals. The radicals themselves have scant interest in departure. I would personally love to end my days on this new planet Rustum, deep though my roots are here, but who would come with me?

'Therefore, Saburo, we can only endure until …'

Anker's hands fell off the keys. The pain through his breast seemed to rip it open.

He stood up, somehow, clawing for air. Or his body did. His mind was suddenly remote, knowing it had perhaps a

24

minute to look down upon the fjord and out to the sky. And he said to himself, with a strange thankful joy, the promise three thousand years old, Odysseus, death will come to you out of the sea, death in his gentlest guise.

4

Everybody knew Jan Svoboda was estranged from his father, the Commissioner. But no orders for his arrest, or even his harassment, had ever come, so presumably an eventual reconciliation was possible. This would in fact, if not officially, re-elevate the young Citizen to Guardian status. Therefore it was advisable to stay on the right side of him.

And thus Jan Svoboda could never be sure how much of his rise was due to himself and how much to some would-be sycophant in the Oceanic Minerals office. With few exceptions, he could not even be sure how many of his friends really meant it. Nor did his attempts to find out, or his occasional blunt questions, lead anywhere. Obviously not. He became a bitter man.

His father's educational decree provoked a tirade from him which brought envy to the eyes of his fellow Constitutionalists. They would have liked to make those remarks, but they weren't Commissioners' sons. Their own formal appeals were denied, and they settled down to make the best of a foul situation. After all, they were a literate, well-to-do, pragmatically oriented class; they could give supplemental instruction at home, or even hire tutors.

The new system was established. A year passed.

On a gusty fall evening, Jan Svoboda set his aircar down at home. Great gray waves marched from the west and roared among the house caissons. Their spume and spindrift went over the roof. The sky streamed past, low and ragged. Visibility was so narrow that he could see no other houses whatsoever.

Which suited him, he thought. A sea dwelling was expensive, and though well paid, he could only afford this one because a Constitutionalist normally led a quiet life. Even so, he felt the financial pinch. But where else could a man live these days within a horizon uncluttered by oafs?

His car touched wheels to the main deck, the garage door opened for him and closed behind, he got out into an insulated stillness. Faintly came a whisper that was gymbal mountings, gyrostabilizers, air conditioner, power plant; louder, though also hushed, were the hoot of wind and the ocean where it brawled. He had a wish to step out and take the cold wet air in his face. Those idiots in the office today, couldn't they see that the ion exchange system now in use was inefficient at tropical concentrations and a little basic research could produce a design which – Svoboda hit the car with a knotted fist. It was no use. There was nothing to fight. You might as well try to catch water in a net.

He sighed and entered the kitchen: a medium-sized, rather slender man, dark, with high cheekbones and hooked nose and a deep, premature wrinkle between his eyes.

'Hullo, darling.' His wife gave him a kiss. 'Ouch,' she added. 'That was like bussing a brick wall. What happened?'

'The usual,' grunted Svoboda. He heard startling silence. 'Where're the kids?'

'Jocelyn called from the mainland and said she wanted to stay overnight with a girl friend. I said okay.'

Svoboda stopped. He stared at her for a long time. Judith took a backward step. 'Why, what's the matter?' she asked.

'What's the matter?' His voice rose as he spoke. 'Do you realize that she and I broke off yesterday in the middle of the conformal-mapping theorem? She seems plain unable to get it through her head. No wonder, with her whole day at school given to Homemaking or some such ridiculous thing, as if her only choice in life fell between being a rich man's toy or a poor man's slave. And how do you expect she'll ever be able to think straight, without knowing how language functions? Great horny toads! By tomorrow night she'll have forgotten everything I did get her to understand yesterday!'

Svoboda grew aware he was shouting. He stopped, swallowed, and considered the situation objectively. 'I'm sorry,' he said. 'Shouldn't have blown my top like that. You didn't know.'

'Perhaps I did,' said Judith slowly.

'What?' Svoboda, who had been leaving the kitchen, spun on his heel.

She braced herself and told him: 'There's more to life than discipline. You can't expect healthy youngsters to go to school on the mainland four days a week, six hours a day, meeting other children who *live* there, hearing games planned, excursions, parties – after school – and then return here, where there isn't anyone their age, nothing but your lessons and your books.'

'We go sailing,' he argued, taken aback. 'Diving, fishing ... visiting.... The Lochabers have a boy David's age, and the de Smets—'

'We see those people maybe once a month,' interrupted Judith. 'Josy's and Davy's friends are on the mainland.'

'Fine lot of friends,' snapped Svoboda. 'Who's Josy staying with?' She hesitated. 'Well?'

'She didn't say.'

He nodded, stiff in the neck muscles. 'I thought so. You see, we're old fogies. We wouldn't approve of a fourteen-year-old girl at a harmless little marijuana party. If that's all they have planned.' He shouted again: 'Well, this is the last time it happens! Any more such requests are to be turned down flat, and hell take their precious social lives!'

Judith caught a shaky lower lip between her teeth. She looked away from him and said, 'It was so different last year.'

'Of course it was. We had our own schools then. No need for extra instruction at home; the right things were taught during the regular hours. No need to worry about their schoolmates: our kind of kids; with decent behavior and sensible prestige symbols. But now, what can we do?'

Svoboda passed a hand across his eyes. His head ached. Judith came over and rubbed her cheek across his breast. 'Don't take it so hard, sweetheart,' she murmured. 'Remember what Laird used to say. "Cooperate with the inevitable."

'You're omitting what he meant by "cooperate," ' replied Svoboda gloomily. 'He meant to use the inevitable the way a judo master uses his opponent's attack. We're forgetting his advice, all of us are forgetting, now that he's gone.'

She held him close for a wordless minute. The glory came back; he looked beyond the wall and breathed, 'You don't know what it was like. You were too young, you didn't enter the movement till Laird was dead. I was only a kid myself, and my father jeered at him. But I saw the man speak, both video and live, and even then I knew. Not that I really understood. But I knew here was a tall man with a beautiful voice, talking about hope to people whose kin lay dead in bombed-out houses. I think afterward, when I began to study the theory behind Constitutionalism, I was trying to get back the feeling I had then.... And my father could do nothing but make fun of him!' He stopped. 'I'm sorry, dear. You've heard this from me a hundred times.'

'And Laird is gone,' she sighed.

He blurted in reborn anger what he had never told her before: 'Murdered. I'm sure of it. Not just by some chance-met Brother on a dark street – no, I got a word here, a hint there, my father had spoken privately to Laird, Laird had grown too big – I accused him to his face of having had Laird done away with. He grinned and did not deny it. That was when I left him. And now he's trying to murder Laird's work!'

He tore free of her and stormed from the kitchen, through the dining room and living room on his way out. A taste of the gale might cool the boiling in him.

On the living room floor, his son David sat cross-legged, swaying with half-shut eyes.

Svoboda halted. He was not noticed.

'What are you doing?' he said at last.

The nine-year-old countenance turned up to him, briefly dazed as if wakened from sleep. 'Oh ... hello, sir.'

'I asked what you were doing,' rapped Svoboda.

David's lids drooped. Looking from beneath them, he had a curious sly appearance. 'Homework,' he muttered.

'What the devil kind of homework is that? And since when has that flatheaded wretch of a teacher made any demand on your intellect?'

'We're to practice, sir.'

'Quit evading me!' Svoboda planted himself above the boy, fists on hips, and glared down. 'Practice what?'

David's expression approached the mutinous, but he seemed to decide on cooperation. 'El ... el ... elementary attunement,' he said. 'Jus' to get the technique. You need years to have the, the ack-shual experience.'

'Attunement? Experience?' Svoboda had again the sense of trying to net a river. 'Explain yourself. Attunement to what?'

David flushed. 'The Ineffable All.' It was a defiance.

'Now wait,' said Svoboda, fighting for calm. 'You're in a secular school. By law. You're not being taught a religion, are you?' For a moment, he hoped so. If the government ever started favoring one of the million cults and creeds over another, it would guarantee trouble – which might make a wedge for —

'Oh, no, sir. This is fact. Mr. Tse explained.'

Svoboda sat down on the floor beside his son. 'What kind of fact?' he asked. 'Scientific?'

'No. No, not eggzackly. You tol' me yourself, science don't have all the answers.'

'Doesn't,' corrected Svoboda mechanically. 'Agreed. To maintain that it does is equivalent to maintaining that the discovery of structured data is the sum total of human experience: which is a self-evident absurdity.' He felt pleased at the easiness of his tone. There was some childish misunderstanding here, which could be cleared up with sensible talk. Looking down on the curly brown head, Svoboda was almost overwhelmed by tenderness. He wanted to rumple the boy's hair and invite him to the sunporch for a game of catch. However —

'In normal usage,' he explained, 'the word "fact" is reserved for empirical data and well-confirmed theories. This Ineffable All is an obvious metaphor. It's like when you say you're full up to the ears with food. A way of talking, not a fact. You must mean you're studying something about esthetics: what makes a picture nice to look at, and so on.'

'Oh, no, sir.' David shook his head vigorously. 'It's *true*. A higher truth than science.'

'But then you are speaking of religion!'

'No, sir. Mr. Tse told us about it. The older kids at school are already in, uh, a little bit in attunement. I mean, by this sort of exercise you don't just ap, ap, apprehend the All. You become the All. You aren't every day, I mean —'

Svoboda leaped back to his feet. David stared. The father said in a voice that shook: 'What sort of nonsense is this? What do those words All and Attunement mean? What structure has this identification, which is somehow only an identification on alternate Thursdays, got? Go on! You know enough basic semantics to explain. You can at least show me where definitions fail and ostensive experience takes over. Go on, tell me!'

David sprang up too. His hands were clenched at his sides and tears stood in his eyes. 'That don't mean anything!' he yelled. 'You don't! Mr. Tse says you don't! He says this playing with words and d-definitions, logic, it's a lotta hooey! He says it's down on the ma-material plane. Attunement's real. This ole science isn't real. You're holding me back with your ole logic and, and, and the big kids laughed at me! I don't want to study your ole semantics. I don't want to. I won't!'

Svoboda regarded him for an entire minute. Then he strode back through the kitchen. 'I'm going out,' he said. 'Don't wait up for me.' The door to the garage shut behind him. Moments afterward, Judith heard his car take off into the storm.

5

Theron Wolfe shook his head. 'Tsk-tsk-tsk,' he chided. 'Temper, temper.'

'Don't tell me it's immature to get angry,' said Jan Svoboda in a dull tone. 'Anker never wrote any such thing. Laird said once it was nonsane not to get angry, in atrocious situations.'

'Agreed,' said Wolfe. 'And no doubt you relieved your glands considerably by flying to the mainland, storming into poor little Tse's one-room apartment, and beating him up before the eyes of his wife and children. I don't see that you accomplished much else, though. Come on, let's get out of here.'

They left the jail. A respectful policeman bowed them toward Wolfe's car. 'Sorry about our mistake, sir,' he said.

'That's okay,' said Wolfe. 'You had to arrest him, since he was not doing his brawling in Lowlevel and you did not know he was the Psychologics Commissioner's son.' Svoboda curled a weary lip. 'But you did well to call me as he insisted.'

'Do you wish to file any charges against the Tse person?' asked the officer. 'We'll take care of him, sir.'

'No,' said Svoboda.

'You might even send him some flowers, Jan,' suggested Wolfe. 'He's only a hack, executing his orders.'

'He doesn't have to be a hack,' Svoboda barked. 'I'm sick of this whine, "Don't blame me, blame the system." There isn't any system: there are men, who act well or badly.'

Wolfe's Jovian form preceded him into the car. The merchant took the controls and they murmured along the ramp and into the air. It was still night, still windy. The jeweled web of Highlevel illumination stretched thin above Lowlevel darkness. Near the eastern horizon, a hunchbacked moon sent flickers of light off a black restless Atlantic.

'I had your car sent to my place, and shot Judith a message so she won't worry,' said Wolfe. 'Instead of rousing her when you stumble in, how about staying overnight with me and taking a holiday tomorrow? You need to unkink.'

'All right.' Svoboda slumped.

Wolfe put the autopilot on Cruise, offered a cigar, and struck one for himself. Its red glow as he sucked sketched his features upon shadow, a bearded Buddha with a faint smile of Mephistopheles. 'Look here,' he said, 'you were always a hairtrigger type, but basically levelheaded. Otherwise you wouldn't be a Constitutionalist. Let's examine the situation objectively. Why do you care what your children become? I mean, naturally you want them to be happy and so on, but does it have to be your kind of happiness?'

'Let's not get into the hedonistic fallacy,' said Svoboda with a tired annoyance. 'I want my kids to become the right sort of human adults.'

'In other words, not only individuals, but cultures have an instinct to survive,' said Wolfe. 'Very good. I agree with you. Our particular culture, yours and mine, emphasizes the conscious mind – perhaps too much for perfect health, but still we think we've potentially got the best way to live. It's being swallowed up by a new culture which exalts a set of as-yet-undefined subconscious and visceral functions. So we're like the Jewish Zealots, English Puritans, Russian Old Believers, any sect trying to restore certain basics that its members feel have been corrupted. (And actually, like the others, we're creating something altogether new; but let's not dim that fine fresh purposefulness of yours with too much analysis.) Also like them, we're more and more at odds with the surrounding society. At the same time, our beliefs are becoming popular with a certain class of people, throughout the world. This in turn alarms the custodians of things-as-they-are. They act to curb our influence. We react. Friction increases.'

'Well?' said Svoboda.

'Well,' said Wolfe, 'I don't see how we can avoid the continued exacerbation of the conflict; and physical force remains the *ultima ratio*. But I don't advise putting well-meaning little teachers in the hospital.'

Svoboda sat straight with a jerk. 'You don't mean another rebellion?' he exclaimed.

'Not like the last fiasco,' said Wolfe. 'Let's not end up like the Old Believers. The Puritan Commonwealth is the analogy we desire. It'll take patience ... yes, and prudence, my friend. What we must do is organize. Not too formally, but we must be able to act as a group. It won't be hard to achieve that much; you aren't the only man who resents what's being done to his children. Once organized, we can start making our weight felt. Boycotts, for instance; bribes to the right officials; and please don't look shocked when I put out that Lowlevel is full of skilled assassins with very reasonable fees.'

'I see.' Svoboda was calmer now. 'Pressure. Yes. We may be able to get our schools restored, if nothing else.'

'Pressure will provoke counter-pressure, though. This will force us to push harder yet. The possible, even probable end result is war.'

'What? No!'

'Or a *coup d'état*. Most likely civil war, however. Since a few military and police officers already subscribe to constitutionalism, and we can hope to recruit more, we've a chance to win. If we proceed with care. This can't be hurried. But ... we might start quietly caching weapons.'

Again Svoboda was jarred. He had seen dead men in the streets when he was a child. Next time there might even be the ultimate violence of the nuclear bomb or the artificial plague. And how much rebuilding would be possible afterward, on this impoverished globe?

'We've got to find another way,' he whispered. 'We can't let matters go that far.'

'We may have to,' said Wolfe. 'We will certainly have to threaten to. Or else go under.'

34

He glanced at the profile beside him, sharp against the stars. Even as he watched, it stiffened with a resolution which, nourished, could become fanaticism. Wolfe almost declared what was really in his mind, but stopped himself.

6

Commissioner Svoboda looked at the clock. 'Get out,' he said. 'The whole lot of you.'

The guards obeyed in surprise. Only Iyeyasu remained; that went without saying. For a moment the big office was quiet.

'Your son comes now, yes?' asked the Okinawan.

'In five minutes,' said Svoboda. 'He'll be prompt, if I know him. To be sure, men change, and we haven't spoken for a good many years.'

He felt a nervous tic in the corner of his mouth. It wouldn't stop, damn it, damn to the seventh circle of Dante's imagination, calm down, will you? The dwarfish man scrambled from his chair and limped across to the full-wall transparency. The towers and ways shimmered below him, heated, but winter lay in pale sky and remote-looking frosty sun. A late winter this year. Svoboda wondered if it would ever end.

Not that the season mattered, when your life ran out in offices. But he would like to see the cherry orchard that crowned this building bloom once more. He had never allowed the roof to be greenhoused. Let's keep a remnant of unscientific nature in the world.

'I wonder if that's why technological civilization is dying,' he mused. 'The reason may not be loss of resources, or the uncontrolled obsession to reproduce, or the decline of literacy, or the rise of mysticism, or any such thing. Those may be mere effects, and the real cause be a collective unconscious revolt against this steel and machinery. If we evolved among forests, do we dare cut down every tree on Earth?'

Iyeyasu didn't answer. He was used to his master's moods. He looked at him with compassionate small eyes.

'If this be so,' said Svoboda, 'then perhaps my maneuverings have served no ultimate purpose. But come, we Practical Men have no time to stop and think.'

The sardonicism uplifted him. He went back and sat down behind his desk and waited, a cigaret between his fingers.

The door opened for Jan on the stroke of 0900. Svoboda's first shocked thought was *Bernice*. Oh, God, he had forgotten how the boy had Bernice's eyes, and she fifteen years in the earth. He sat for a moment in an aloneness that stung.

'Well?' said Jan coldly.

Svoboda braced his thin shoulders. 'Sit down,' he invited.

Jan perched on a chair's edge and stared across the desk. He had grown thinner, his father noticed, and tense, but the youthful awkwardness was gone. An uncompromising harsh face jutted above that plain blue tunic.

'Smoke?' asked the Commissioner.

'No,' said Jan.

'I hope everything is all right at home? Your wife? Your children?' *Most men are privileged to see their own grandchildren. Ah, stop sniveling, you tinpot Machiavelli.*

'We are in physical health,' said Jan. His voice was like iron. 'You are a busy man, Commissioner. I don't wish to take up your time unduly.'

'No, I suppose not.' Svoboda put another cigaret between his lips, remembered he was still holding the first, and ground it out with needless violence. Self-control returned, to parch his tones. 'I imagine when the question first arose of a conference between myself and a representative of your new Constitutionalist Association, it seemed most natural for me to see your president, Mr. Wolfe. You may wonder why I specified you instead, who are only the engineering member of your policy committee.'

Jan's mouth tightened. 'I hope you did not plan an emotional appeal.'

'Oh, no. The fact is, Wolfe and I have already had several discussions.' Svoboda chuckled. 'Ah-ha. That startled you, eh? Now if I were determined to wreck your organization, I would let you stew over the fact. But the truth is merely that Wolfe talked to me on the 'phone, unofficially, and sounded me out on various points. Of course, that entailed me sounding him out too, but we reached a tacit agreement.'

Svoboda leaned on his elbows, puffed smoke, and went on: 'Your organization was formed several months ago. Constitutionalists have been joining it by thousands, everywhere in the world. What they want from it varies. Some want a spokesman for their grievances; some, doubtless, a revolutionary underground; the majority probably have no more than vague expectations of mutual help. Since you have not yet adopted any clear-cut program, you have disappointed no one. But now your committee must soon come up with a definite plan of action, or see the outfit revert to primordial jelly.'

'We've got a plan,' his son retorted. 'Since you know so much, I can tell you what our first step will be. We're going to make a formal petition for repeal of your so-called educational decree. We're not without influence on several of your fellow Commissioners. If the petition is denied, we'll call for stronger measures.'

'The economic squeeze.' Svoboda's large bald head nodded. 'Boycotts and slowdowns. If that fails, strikes, disguised as mass resignation. The next resort, no doubt, civil disobedience. Thereafter — Oh, well. The pattern is classic.'

'Classic because it works,' said Jan. The blood crept up his cheeks, making him heartbreakingly boylike again.

'Sometimes.'

'You could save everyone a lot of trouble by cancelling the decree at once. In that case, we might be willing to compromise on a few other points.'

'Oh, but I'm not going to.' Svoboda folded his hands as if in prayer, rolled his eyes heavenward, and chanted piously around his cigaret, 'The public interest demands the public school.'

Jan jumped erect. 'You know that's only a hypocritical way of destroying us!'

'As a matter of fact,' said Svoboda, 'I plan to have the curriculum modified next fall. The time now devoted to critical analysis of literary works could better be spent in rote memorization. And then, with hallucinogens becoming so important socially, a practical course in their proper use—'

'You shriveled-up son of a sewer!' screamed Jan. He lunged across the desk.

Iyeyasu was there without seeming to cross the floor between. The edge of a hand cracked down on Jan's wrist. The other hand, stiff-fingered, poked him in the solar plexus. Jan gasped out his wind and collapsed backward.

'Careful, there,' warned Svoboda. His knuckles turned white where he gripped the desk.

'No harm done, sir,' Iyeyasu assured him. He eased Jan into the chair and began kneading his shoulders and the base of his skull. 'He gets air back in a minute.' With an ill-concealed rage: 'Is not a way to speak to your father.'

'For all I know,' said Svoboda, 'he may have been correct.'

The glaze left Jan's eyes, but no one talked for a while. Svoboda lit another cigaret and stared into space. He wanted to look at the boy, there might never be another chance, but it would be poor tactics. Jan slumped under Iyeyasu's mountainous form. At last he spoke, sullenly:

'I don't apologize. What else could you expect?'

'Nothing, perhaps.' Svoboda made a bridge of his fingers and regarded his son across them. 'There will certainly be resistance to such measures. And yet I'm only underlining a conflict which would otherwise proceed more slowly but to the same inevitable end. You did not let me explain why you, rather than Wolfe, are your people's representative today. The fact is that you are young and hot headed, a much better spokesman for the upcoming Constitutionalist generation, than an older, more cautious, less indoctrinated man. The extremists in your party might repudiate any compromise agreement made by Wolfe, simply because he is Wolfe, notoriously all things to all men. But if you endorse a plan, they will listen.'

'What agreement can we make?' Jan snarled. 'Unless you return us our children —'

'No maudlin figures of speech, please. Let me explain the difficulty. You and the government represent opposing ways of life. They simply cannot be reconciled. Once, perhaps, there was a possibility of coexistence. There may be again in the future, when the issues no longer seem vital. But not now. Just suppose that we did give in, repealed the educational decree and reinstated your system of private schools. It would be a victory for you and a defeat for us. You would gain not only your immediate objective, but confidence, support, strength. We would lose correspondingly. How long before you made your next demand? You have other grudges besides this. Having gotten back your schools, you may next want back the right to criticize political basics. If you gain that, you will want the right to agitate publicly. Having gotten that, you will want representation on the Commission. Then — But I need not elaborate. It seems best to settle the matter now, once and forever, before you get too strong. And that's why you won't get as much support from my colleagues as you expect.'

Jan bristled. 'If you think this is the final word —'

'Oh, no. We've already discussed the means by which you'll apply pressure. I am also well aware of your potential for accumulating weapons, subverting military units, and eventually resorting to force. A number of Guardians want to arrest the bunch of you at once. But alas, you are too important. Imagine the chaos if a fourth of the technical personnel in Minerals or Pelagiculture vanished, without leaving trained successors. Or if Wolfe was suddenly removed from his devious routes of supply, where would half the mistresses on Highlevel get new gowns to outshine the other half? Then, also, it's a truism that martyrs are a stimulant to any cause. There would be plenty of young men who had never cared one way or another about your philosophy, suddenly fired by the vision of a thing bigger than themselves.... Yes, by acting too strongly we might provoke the very war we were trying to forestall.'

Svoboda leaned back. He had the boy on the ropes now, he saw: bewildered gaze, half-parted lips, a hand raised as if uncertain whether to defend or appeal or offer thanks.

'There is a possible compromise,' he said.

'What?' Jan's question was barely audible.

'Rustum. E Eridani II.'

'The new planet?' Jan's head snapped up. 'But —'

'If the most dissatisfied Constitutionalists left Earth voluntarily, after making proper arrangements for replacement personnel and so on, the pressure would be off us. Then, in time, we could back down on the school issue and please your stay-at-home friends, without actually being defeated on it. Or, even if we didn't, *you* would be quit of us; and we'd be quit of the most stubborn element of our opposition. The successful planting of the colony would be kudos for the whole Commission, a shot in the buttocks for space travel, and therefore well worth our support and encouragement. As for the considerable expense involved – you people own valuable property which couldn't be taken with you, so by selling out you can finance the project.

'It's an old pattern in history. Massachusetts, Maryland, Pennsylvania were promoted by a government hostile to the ideals involved and anxious to get rid of the idealists. Why not a repeat performance?'

'But twenty light-years,' whispered Jan. 'Never to see Earth again.'

'You'll have to give up a lot,' agreed Svoboda. 'But in return, you'll escape the risk of destruction by force or absorption by my evil schemes.' He shrugged. 'Of course, if your nice radiant-heated sea house is more important than your philosophy, by all means stay home.'

Jan shook his head, as if he had taken a fresh blow. 'I'll have to think about it,' he mumbled.

'Consult Wolfe,' said Svoboda. 'He knows about this. He broached the idea to me.'

'What?' The eyes that were Bernice's grew candid with

surprise.

'I told you Wolfe is not a fire-eater,' Svoboda laughed. 'I gather he's discussed the possibility of overthrowing the government, and done some preliminary organizing for that purpose. But I suspect it was never his real intention. That was mere window dressing, for the benefit of people whose enthusiasm needed whipping up. He's been working toward a strong bargaining position ... so he can make us send you to Rustum.'

This was the right note, he saw. If Wolfe the mentor had been operating behind the scenes, Jan would have less fear of a bomb in any final agreement reached.

'I'll have to talk to him.' The boy rose. He was suddenly trembling. 'To all of them. We'll have to think – Goodbye.'

He turned and stumbled toward the door.

'Goodbye, kid,' said Svoboda.

He doubted if Jan heard him. The door closed.

Svoboda sat without moving for a long time. The cigaret between his fingers burned so low that it scorched him. He swore, dropped it in the disposer, and struggled to his feet. The broken foot was hurting him again.

Iyeyasu glided around the desk. Svoboda leaned on the tree-trunk arm, shuffling to the clear wall until he could stare out and catch a glitter of open ocean.

'Your son comes back, yes?' asked Iyeyasu finally.

'I don't expect so,' answered Svoboda.

'You wanting them go to the planet?'

'Yes. And they will. I haven't been working these many years without getting to know my machinery.'

The sun out there was pale, but its light stung Svoboda's eyes so he had to rub them with a knuckle. He said aloud, in a precise but annoyingly unsteady tone: 'Old Inky was an educated man in his way. He used to claim that the main axiom in human geometry is, a straight line is not the shortest distance between two points. In fact, there are no straight lines. I find that's pretty true.'

'This was your plan, sir?' Iyeyasu's voice held more sympathy than intellectual interest.

'Uh-huh. Anker's books, and my own common sense, showed me there was no hope for Earth in the foreseeable future. Maybe when collapse has ended the decadence, a thousand years hence, something will evolve here; but that won't help my son much. I wanted to get him out while there was still time. To a new world for a fresh start. But he couldn't go alone. It would have to be as part of a colony. And the colonists would have to be healthy, independent, able people, who'd gone of their own free will; no other type was likely to survive. I was gambling that a habitable planet would be discovered, but I could not gamble that it would be very hospitable.... But why should such people leave? Civilization hasn't rotted so far that given half a chance, they can't do rather well for themselves here at home.

'So there had to be an obstacle on Earth which sheer drive and intelligence could not overcome. What sort would that be? Well, it's in the nature of intercultural conflicts to be insoluble. When axioms clash, logic is helpless. So I set up a rival society within the Federation. That wasn't hard. Here in North America, a dying culture had just tried to assert itself by rebellion, and failed; but it wasn't dead yet. It did need to be given a new spirit and a sense of direction. I had Anker's philosophy for a background. I had Laird, a marvelous actor with much brains and no conscience. He proved expensive but faithful, since I made it plain what would happen if he wasn't. When his work was finished, I retired him – a new face, a new name, and a lavish pension. He caroused himself to death four years ago. Of course, the possibility that I had had Laird murdered was always left open. The first irritating wound, with many more to follow.'

Svoboda remembered a boy who raged from the house and never came back. He sighed. One can't foresee every detail. At least Bernice's grandchildren would grow up as free people, if Rustum didn't eat them.

'In the end,' he said, 'I'd maneuvered my Constitutionalists into such a position that their own wily Wolfe was bound to maneuver me into helping them emigrate. I think we're over the hump now. We can sit back, you and I, and watch the wagon roll downhill. With stars at the bottom of the hill.'

'We go south,' suggested Iyeyasu clumsily. 'You can watch his new sun.'

'I imagine I'll be dead before he gets there,' said Svoboda. He gnawed his lip a moment, then straightened and hobbled from the window. 'Come on. Let's go visit some fellow Commissioner and be nasty to him.'

Part 2: The Burning Bridge

1

The message was an electronic shout, the most powerful and tightly-beamed shortwave transmission which men could generate, directed with all the precision which mathematics and engineering could offer. Nevertheless that pencil must scrawl broadly over the sky, and for a long time, merely hoping to write on its target. For when distances are measured in light-weeks, the smallest errors grow monstrous.

As it happened, the attempt was successful. Communications Officer Anastas Mardikian had assembled his receiver after acceleration ceased – a big thing, surrounding the flagship *Ranger* like a spiderweb trapping a fly – and had kept it hopefully tuned over a wide band. The radio beam swept through, ghostly faint from dispersion, wave-length doubled by Doppler effect, ragged with cosmic noise. An elaborate system of filters and amplifiers could make it no more than barely intelligible.

But that was enough.

Mardikian burst onto the bridge. He was young, and the months had not yet tarnished the glory of his first deep-space voyage. 'Sir!' he yelled. 'A message ... I just played back the recorder ... a message from Earth!'

Fleet Captain Joshua Coffin started. That movement, in weightlessness, spun him off the deck. He stopped himself with a practiced hand, stiffened, and rapped back: 'If you haven't learned regulations by now, a week of solitary confinement may give you a chance to study them.'

'I ... but, sir —' The other man retreated. His uniform made a loose rainbow splash across metal and plastic. Coffin alone, of the fleet's whole company, held to the black garments of a space service long extinct.

'But, sir,' said Mardikian. 'Word from Earth!'

'Only the duty officer may enter the bridge without permission,' Coffin reminded him. 'If you had anything urgent to tell, there is an intercom.'

'I thought —' choked Mardikian. He paused, then came to the free-fall equivalent of attention. Anger glittered in his eyes. 'Sorry, sir.'

Coffin hung quiet a while, looking at the dark young man in the brilliant clothes. *Forget it*, he said to himself. *Times are another. This is as good as spacemen get to be nowadays, careless, superstitious, jabbering among each other in languages I don't understand. Thank the Lord God there are any recruits whatsoever, and hope He will let there continue to be a few for what remains of your life.*

The duty officer, Hallmyer, was tall and blond and born in Lancashire; but he watched the other two with Asian eyes. No one spoke, though Mardikian breathed heavily. Stars filled the bow viewport, crowding a huge night.

Coffin sighed. 'Very well,' he said. 'I'll let it pass this time.'

After all, he reflected, a message from Earth was an event. Radio had gone between Sol and Alpha Centauri, but that was with very special equipment. To pinpoint a handful of ships, moving at half the speed of light, and to do it so well that the comparatively tiny receiver Mardikian had erected would pick up the beam — Yes, the boy had some excuse for gladness.

'What was the signal?' Coffin inquired.

He expected it would only be routine, a test, so that engineers a lifetime hence could ask the returning fleet whether the transmission had registered. If there were any engineers by then. Instead, Mardikian blurted:

'Old Svoboda is dead. The new Psychologics Commissioner is Thomas ... Thomson ... that part didn't record clearly ... anyway, he must be sympathetic to the Constitutionalists. He's rescinded the educational decree – promised more consideration for provincial mores — Come hear for yourself, sir!'

46

Despite himself, Coffin whistled. 'But that's why the Eridani colony was being founded,' he said. His words fell flat and silly into silence.

Hallmyer said, with the alien hiss in his English that Coffin hated, for it was like the Serpent in a once noble garden:

'Apparently the colony has lost its reason for being started. But how shall we consult with 3000 would-be pioneers lying in deepsleep?'

'Shall we?' Coffin did not know why – not yet – but he felt his brain move with the speed of fear. 'We've undertaken to deliver them to Rustum. In the absence of specific orders from Earth, are we even allowed to consider a change of plans ... since a general vote can't be taken? Better avoid possible trouble and not even mention —' He broke off. Mardikian's face had become a mask of dismay.

'But, sir!' bleated the Com officer.

A chill rose in Coffin. 'You have already told,' he said.

'Yes,' whispered Mardikian. 'I met Coenrad de Smet, he had come over to this ship for some repair parts, and – I never thought —'

'Exactly!' growled Coffin.

2

The fleet numbered fifteen, more than half the inter-stellar ships humankind possessed. It could not cross the six parsecs to e Eridani and return in less than 82 years. But the government didn't mind that. It had even provided speeches and music when the colonists embarked. After which, Coffin thought, it had doubtless grinned to itself and thanked its various heathen gods that that was over with.

'Only now,' he muttered, 'it isn't.'

He free-sat in the *Ranger*'s general room, waiting for the conference to start. The austerity of the walls around him was broken by a few pictures. Coffin had wanted to leave them bare (since no one else would be interested in a photograph of that catboat the boy Joshua had sailed on a Massachusetts bay which glittered in summers now forgotten) – but even the theoretically absolute power of a fleet captain had its limits. At least the men were not making this room obscene with naked women. Though in all honesty, he wasn't sure he wouldn't rather have that than ... brush strokes on rice paper, the suggestion of a tree, and a classic ideogram.... He did not understand the new generations.

The *Ranger* skipper, Nils Kivi, was like a breath of home: a small dapper Finn who had traveled with Coffin on the first e Eridani trip. They were not exactly friends, an admiral has no intimates, but they had been young in the same decade.

Actually, thought Coffin, *most of us spacemen are anachronisms. I could talk to Goldberg or Yamato or Pereira, to quite a few on this voyage, and not meet blank surprise when I mentioned a dead actor or hummed a dead song. But they're in deepsleep now. We'll stand our one-year watches in turn, and be put back in the coldvats, and have no chance to talk till journey's end.*

'It may prove to be fun,' mused Kivi.

'What?' asked Coffin.

'To walk around High America again, and fish in the Emperor River, and dig up our old camp,' said Kivi. 'We had some fine times on Rustum, along with the work and danger.'

Coffin was startled, that his own thoughts should have been so closely followed. 'Yes,' he agreed, remembering strange wild dawns on the Cleft edge, 'that was a pretty good five years.'

Kivi sighed. 'Different this time,' he said. 'Maybe I don't want to go back. We were discoverers then, walking where men had never laid eyes before. Now the colonists will be the hopeful ones. We are nothing but their transportation.'

Coffin shrugged. He had heard the complaint before, even prior to departure and often enough on the voyage so far. Men cooped together like this must learn to endure each other's repetitiousness. 'We must take what is given us, and be thankful,' he said.

'This time,' said Kivi, 'I worry: suppose I come home again and find my job abolished? No more space travel ever. If that happens, I refuse to be thankful.'

Forgive him, Coffin asked his God, Who seldom forgave. *It is cruel to watch the foundation of your life being corroded away.*

Kivi's eyes lit up, the briefest flicker. 'Of course,' he said, 'if we really do cancel this trip and go straight back, we may not arrive too late. We may still find a few expeditions to new stars being organized, and get on their rosters.'

Coffin tautened. Again he was unsure why he felt an emotion: this time, anger. 'I shall permit no disloyalty to the purpose for which we are engaged,' he clipped.

'Oh, come off it,' Kivi said. 'Be rational. I don't know your reason for undertaking this wretched cruise. You had rank enough to turn down the assignment; no one else did. But you want to explore as badly as I. If Earth didn't care about us, they would not have bothered to invite us back. Let us seize the chance while it lasts.' He intercepted a

49

reply by glancing at the wall chrono. 'Time for our conference.' He flicked the intership switch.

A televisual panel came to life, divided into fourteen sections, one for each accompanying vessel. One or two faces peered from each. The craft which bore only supplies and deepsleeping crewmen were represented by their captains. Those which had colonists revealed a civilian spokesman as well as a skipper.

Coffin studied each image in turn. The spacemen he knew. They all belonged to the Society, and even those born long after him had much in common. There was a necessary minimum discipline of mind and body, and the underlying dream for which everything else in life had been traded – new horizons beneath new suns. Not that spacemen indulged in such poetics; they had too much work to do.

The colonists were something else. With them Coffin shared certain things, too. Their background was predominantly North American, they had a scientific habit of thought, they distrusted government as he did. But few Constitutionalists had any religion; those who did were Romish, Jewish, Buddhist, or otherwise foreign to him. All were tainted with the self-indulgence of this era: they had written into their convenant that no law could touch private morals and that free speech was limited only by personal libel. Coffin thought sometimes he would be glad to see the last of them.

'Is everyone prepared?' he began. 'Very well, let's get down to business. It's unfortunate the Com officer gossiped so loosely. He stirred up a hornets' nest' – Coffin saw that few understood the idiom – 'he created discontent which threatens this whole project. We've got to deal with it.'

Coenrad de Smet, colonist aboard the *Scout*, smiled in a peculiarly irritating way. 'You would simply have concealed the fact?' he asked.

'It would have made matters easier,' said Coffin stiffly.

'In other words,' de Smet said, 'you know better what we might want than we do ourselves. That, sir, is the kind of arrogance we hoped to escape. No man has the right to suppress any information bearing on public affairs.'

A low voice, with a touch of laughter, said through a hood: 'And you accuse Captain Coffin of preaching!'

The New Englander's eyes were drawn to her. Not that he could see through the shapeless gown and mask, such as hid the waking women, but he had met Teresa Zeleny on Earth, in the course of preparing for this expedition. Hearing her now was somehow like remembering Indian summer on a wooded hilltop, a century ago.

Involuntarily, his own lips quirked upward. 'Thank you,' he said. 'Do you, Mr. De Smet, know what the deepsleeping colonists might want? Have you any right to decide for *them*? And yet we can't wake them, even the adults, to vote. There simply isn't room. If nothing else, the air regenerators couldn't supply that much oxygen. That's why I felt it best to tell no one, until we were actually at Rustum. Then those who wished could return with the fleet, I suppose.'

'We could rouse them a few at a time, let them vote, and put them back to sleep,' suggested Teresa Zeleny.

'It would take weeks,' said Coffin. 'You should know especially well that metabolism isn't lightly stopped, or easily restored.'

'If you could see my face,' she said, again with a chuckle, 'I would grimace amen. I'm so sick of tending inert human flesh that – well, I'm glad they're only women and girls, because if I also had to massage and inject men I'd take a vow of chastity.'

Coffin blushed, cursed himself for blushing, and hoped she couldn't see it over the telecircuit. He noticed Kivi grin. Damn Kivi!

A young male colonist added some joke about his task being a sure cure for homosexual tendencies. Coffin fumbled miserably after words. These people were without shame. Here in the great night of God they said things which should have brought thunderbolts, and he had to sit and listen.

Kivi provided the merciful interruption. 'Your few-at-a-time proposal is pointless anyhow,' he said. 'In the course of those weeks we would pass the critical date.'

'What's that?' asked a girl's voice.

'You don't know?' said Coffin, surprised.

'Let it pass for now,' broke in Teresa. Once again, as several times before, Coffin admired her decisiveness. She cut through nonsense with a man's speed and a woman's practicality. 'Take our word, June, that if we don't turn about within two months, we'll do better to go to Rustum. So, voting is out. We could wake a few sleepers but those already conscious are really as adequate a statistical sample.'

Coffin nodded. She spoke for five women on her ship, who stood a year-watch caring for 295 in suspended animation. In the course of the voyage, only 120 would not be restimulated for such duty, and these were children. The proportion on the other nine colonist-laden vessels was similar, while the crew totaled 1620 with 45 up and about at any given time. Whether the die was cast by less than two percent, or by four or five percent, was hardly significant.

'Let's recollect exactly what the message was,' said Coffin. 'The educational decree which directly threatened your Constitutionalist way of life has been withdrawn. You're no worse off than formerly – and no better, though the message hints at further concessions in the future. You're invited home again. That's all. We haven't picked up any other transmissions. It seems very little data on which to base so large a decision.'

'It's an even bigger one to continue,' said de Smet. He leaned forward, a bulky man, until he filled his screen. Hardness rang in his tones. 'We were able people, economically rather well off. I daresay Earth already misses our services, especially in technological fields. Your own report makes Rustum out a grim place. Many of us would die there. Why should we not turn home if we can?'

'Home,' whispered someone.

The word filled a sudden quietness, like water filling a cup, until quietness brimmed over with it. Coffin sat listening to the voice of his ship, generators, ventilators, regulators, and he began to hear a beat frequency which was *Home, home, home.*

Only his home was gone. His father's church was torn down for an Oriental temple, and the woods where October had burned were cleared for another tentacle of city, and the bay was enclosed to make a plankton farm. For him, only a spaceship remained, and the somehow cold hope of heaven.

A very young man said, almost to himself: 'I left a girl back there.'

'I had my personal sub,' said another. 'I used to poke around the Great Barrier Reef, skindiving out the airlock or loafing on the surface. You wouldn't believe how blue the waves could be. They tell me on Rustum you can't come down off the mountaintops.'

'But we'd have the whole planet to ourselves,' said Teresa Zeleny.

One with a gentle scholar's face answered: 'That may be precisely the trouble, my dear. Three thousand of us, counting children, totally isolated from the human mainstream. Can we hope to build a civilization? Or even maintain one?'

'Your problem, pop,' said the officer beside him dryly, 'is that there are no medieval manuscripts on Rustum.'

'I admit it,' said the scholar. 'I thought it more important that my children grow up able to use their minds. But if it turns out they can do so on Earth.... How much chance will the first generations on Rustum have to sit down and really think, anyway?'

'Would there even be a next generation on Rustum?'

'One and a quarter gravities – God! I can feel it now.'

'Synthetics, year after year of synthetics and hydroponics, till we can establish an ecology. I had steak on Earth, once in a while.'

'My mother couldn't come. Too frail. But she's paid for a hundred years of deepsleep, all she could afford ... just in case I do return.'

'I designed skyhouses. They won't build anything on Rustum much better than log cabins, in my lifetime.'

'Do you remember moonlight on the Grand Canyon?'

'Do you remember Beethoven's Ninth in the Federal Concert Hall?'

'Do you remember that funny old tavern on Midlevel, where we drank beer and sang *Lieder*?'

'Do you remember?'

'Do you remember?'

Teresa Zeleny shouted across their voices: 'In Anker's name! What are you thinking about? If you care so little, you should never have embarked in the first place!'

It brought back the silence, not at once but piece by piece, until Coffin could pound the table and call for order. He looked straight at her hidden eyes and said, 'Thank you, Miss Zeleny. I was expecting tears to be uncorked any moment.'

One of the girls snuffed behind her mask.

Charles Lochaber, speaking for the *Courier* colonists, nodded. 'Aye, 'tis a blow to our purpose. I'm not so sairtain I myself would vote to continue, did I feel the message was to be trusted.'

'What?' De Smet's square head jerked up from between his shoulders.

Lochaber grinned without much humor. 'The government has been getting more arbitrary each year,' he said. 'They were ready enough to let us go, aye. But they may regret it now – not because we could ever be an active threat, but because we will be a subversive example, up there in Earth's sky. Or simply because we will *be*. Mind ye, I know not for sairtain; but it's possible they decided we are safer dead, and this is to trick us back. 'Twould be characteristic dictatorship behavior.'

'Of all the fantastic —' gasped an indignant female voice.

'Not as wild as you might think, dear,' Teresa said. 'I've read some history, and I don't mean that censored pap which passes for history nowadays. But there's another possibility just as alarming. That message may be perfectly

54

sincere. But will it still be true when we get back? Remember how long that will take. And even if we could return overnight, to an Earth that welcomed us, what guarantee would there be that our children, or our grandchildren, won't suffer the same troubles as we've had, without the same chance to break free?'

'Ye vote, then, to carry on?' asked Lochaber.

'I do.'

'Good lass. I'm with ye.'

Kivi raised his hand. Coffin recognized him. 'I'm not sure the crew ought not to have a voice in this also,' he said.

'What?' De Smet grew red. He gobbled for a moment before he could get out: 'Do you seriously think you could elect us to settle on that annex of hell – and then come home to Earth yourselves?'

'As a matter of fact,' Kivi smiled, 'I suspect the crew would prefer to return at once. I know I would.'

'I've explained how shortsighted that would be, from your own viewpoint,' said Coffin. 'Space travel has never shown a financial profit. It's always been a scientific venture, an exploration – an ideal, if you like. It won't survive unless people are interested in supporting it. A successful colony on Rustum will provide the inspiration which Earth needs to keep on sending out explorers.'

'That's your opinion,' said Kivi.

'I hope you realize,' said the very young man with ornate sarcasm, 'that every second we sit here arguing takes us 150,000 kilometers further from home.'

'Dinna fash yourself,' said Lochaber. 'Whatever we do, that girl of yours will be an old carline before you reach Earth.'

De Smet was still choking at Kivi: 'You lousy ferryman, if you think you can make pawns of us —'

And Kivi snapped back, 'If you don't watch your language, clodhugger, I will come over there and stuff you down your own throat.'

'Order!' cried Coffin. 'Order!'

Teresa echoed him: 'Please ... for all our lives' sake ...

55

don't you know where we are? You've got a few centimeters of wall between you and zero! Please, we can't fight or we'll never see any planet again.'

But she did not say it weeping, or as a beggary. It was almost a mother's voice (strange, in an unmarried woman) and it quieted the male snarling more than Coffin's shouts.

The fleet captain said finally: 'That will do. Everybody's too worked up to think. Debate is adjourned for four duty periods, sixteen hours. Discuss the problem with your shipmates, get some sleep, and report the consensus at the next meeting.'

'*Sixteen hours?*' yelped someone. 'Do you know how much return time that adds?'

'You heard me,' said Coffin. 'Anyone who wants to argue may do so from the brig. Dismissed!'

He snapped off the screen switch.

Kivi, temper eased, gave him a slow confidential grin. 'That heavy-father act works nearly every time, no?'

Coffin pushed from the table. 'I'm going out,' he said. His voice sounded harsh to him, unfamiliar. 'Carry on.'

He had never felt so alone before, not even the night his father died. *O God, Who spake unto Moses in the wilderness, reveal now Thy will.* But God was silent, and Coffin turned blindly to the only other help he could think of.

3

Space armored, he paused a moment in the airlock before continuing. He had been an astronaut for twenty-five years – for a century if you added time in the vats – but he could still not look upon naked creation without fear.

An infinite blackness flashed: stars beyond stars, to the bright cataract of the Milky Way and on out to other galaxies and flocks of galaxies, until the light which a telescope might now register had been born before the Earth. Looking from his airlock cave, past the radio web and the other ships, Coffin felt himself drown in enormousness, coldness, and total silence. But he knew that this vacuum burned and roared with lethal energies, roiled with currents of gas and dust more massive than planets, and travailed with the birth of new suns; and he said to himself the most dreadful of names, *I am that I am*, and sweat formed chilly globules under his arms.

This much a man could see within the Solar System. Traveling at half light-speed stretched the human mind still further, until often it ripped across and another lunatic was shoved into deepsleep. For aberration redrew the sky, crowding stars toward the bows, so that the ships plunged at a cloud of Doppler hell-blue. The constellations lay thinly abeam; you looked out into the dark. Aft, Sol was still the brightest object in heaven, but it had gained a sullen red tinge, as if already grown old, as if the prodigal would return from far places to find his home buried under ice.

What is man that Thou art mindful of him? The line gave its accustomed comfort; for the Sun-maker had also wrought this flesh, atom by atom, and at the very least would think the soul worthy of hell. Coffin had never understood how his atheist colleagues endured free space.

Well —

He took aim at the next hull and fired his little spring-powered crossbow. A light line unreeled behind the magnetic bolt. He tested its security with habitual care, pulled himself along until he had reached the other ship, yanked the bolt loose and fired again, and so on from hull to slowly orbiting hull, until he reached the *Pioneer*.

Its awkward ugly shape was like a protective wall against the stars. Coffin drew himself past the ion tubes, now cold. Their skeletal structure seemed impossibly frail to have hurled forth peeled atoms at $\frac{1}{2}c$. Mass tanks bulked around the vessel. Allowing for deceleration, plus a small margin, the mass ratio was about nine to one, nine tons expelled for each ton that went to e Eridani. Months would be required at Rustum to refine enough reaction material for the voyage home. Meanwhile, such of the crew as weren't producing it would help the colony get established.

If the colony ever did.

Coffin reached the forward airlock and pressed the 'doorbell.' The outer valve opened for him and he cycled through. First Officer Karamchand met him and helped him doff armor. The other man on duty found an excuse to approach and listen, for monotony was as corrosive out here as distance and strangeness.

'Ah, sir. What brings you over?'

Coffin braced himself. Embarrassment roughened his tone: 'I want to see Miss Zeleny.'

'Of course.... But why come yourself? I mean, the tele-circuit —'

'In person!' barked Coffin.

'What?' escaped the crewman. He propelled himself backward in terror of a wigging. Coffin ignored him.

'Emergency,' he snapped. 'Please intercom her and arrange for a private discussion.'

'Why ... why ... yes, sir. At once. Will you wait here ... I mean ... yes, sir!' Karamchand shot down the corridor.

Coffin felt a sour smile on his own lips. He could sympathize with the men's confusion. His own law about the women had been like steel, and now he violated it himself.

58

The trouble was, he thought, no one knew if it was even required. Hitherto there had been few enough women crossing space, and they only within the Solar System, on segregated ships. There was no background of interstellar experience. It seemed obvious, though, that a man on his year watch should not be asked to tend deep-sleeping female colonists. (Or vice versa!) And would not waking men and women, freely intermingling, be potentially even more explosive? Coffin had decided that harem-like seclusion was the best approach. Husbands and wives were not to be awake at the same times.

Bad enough for the ordinary male to know that a woman lay within a few kilometers. Bad enough to see her veiled whenever there was a teleconference. (Or did the masks make matters worse, by challenging the imagination? Who knew?) Best seal off the living quarters and coldvat sections of the craft which bore her. Crewmen standing watches on those particular ships had better return to their own vessels to sleep and eat. Do it that way, pray God you were being wise, and hope Satan would not snatch too many opportunities when everyone was roused on Rustum.

Coffin braced his muscles. *The rules wouldn't apply if a large meteor struck us*, he reminded himself. *What has come up is more dangerous than that. So never mind what anyone thinks.*

Karamchand returned to salute him and say breathlessly: 'Miss Zeleny will see you, Captain. This way, if you please.'

'Thanks.' Coffin followed to the main bulkhead. Only the women had a key to its door. But now the door stood ajar. Coffin pushed himself through so hard that he overshot and caromed off the farther wall.

Teresa laughed. She closed the door and locked it. 'Just to make them feel safe out there,' she said. 'Poor well-meaning men! Welcome, Captain.'

He turned about, almost dreading the instant. Her tall form was decent in baggy coveralls, but she had dropped the hood. She wasn't pretty, he supposed: Snub-nosed, square-jawed, verging on spinsterhood. But he had liked her way of smiling.

'I—' He found no words.

'Follow me.' She led him down a short passage, hand-over-hand along the null-gee rungs. 'I've warned the other girls to stay away. You needn't fear being shocked.' At the end of the corridor was a partitioned-off cubicle. Few enough personal goods could be taken along, but she had made this place hers with a painting, a battered Shakespeare, the works of Anker, a microplayer. Her tapes ran to Bach, late Beethoven, and Richard Strauss, music which could be studied endlessly. She took hold of a stanchion and nodded, abruptly growing serious.

'What do you want to see me about, Captain?'

Coffin secured himself by the crook of an arm and stared at his hands. The fingers strained against each other. 'I wish I could give you a clear reply,' he said, low and with difficulty. 'I've never encountered any problem like this before. If it involved only men, I guess I could handle it. But there are women along, and children.'

'And you want a female viewpoint. You're wiser than I had realized. But why me?'

He forced himself to meet her eyes. 'You appear the most sensible of the women awake.'

'Really!' She laughed. 'I appreciate the compliment, but must you deliver it in that parade ground voice, and glare at me to boot? Relax, Captain.' She cocked her head, studying him. 'I've a question for you, too. Several of the girls don't get this business of the critical point. I tried to explain, but I was only an R. N. at home and never did have any mathematical brains, so I'm afraid I muddled it rather. Could you put it in words of one and a half syllables?'

'Do you mean the equal-time point?'

'The Point of No Return, some of them call it.'

'Nonsense! It's only — Well, look at it this way. We accelerated from Sol at one gravity. We dare not apply more acceleration, though we could, because so much equipment aboard has been lightly built to save mass. The coldvats, for example, would collapse and kill the people inside, if we went as high as one-point-five gee. Very well. It took us about 180 days to reach maximum velocity. In the course of that period, we covered not quite one and a half light-months of distance. We will now go free for almost forty years. (Cosmic time, that is. The relativistic clock paradox will make it around 35 years aboard ship. No matter.) At the end of our journey, we'll decelerate at one gee for some 180 days, covering a final light-month and a half, and enter the e Eridani System with low relative speed. Our star-to-star orbit was plotted with care, but of course the unavoidable errors may add up to many Astronomical Units. Furthermore, we have to maneuver, put our ships in orbit around Rustum, send ferry craft back and forth. So we carry a reaction-mass reserve which allows us a total velocity change of about 1000 kilometers per second once we get there.

'Now imagine we'd decided to turn back immediately after reaching full speed. We'd have to decelerate at the same one gee. We'd have been a year in space and almost a quarter light-year from Sol before we achieved relative rest and could start back. To go those three light-months at 1000 K.P.S. takes roughly 72 years. But the whole round trip as originally scheduled, with a one-year layover at Rustum, runs just about 83 years!

'Obviously there's some point in time beyond which we can actually get home quicker by staying with the original plan. This date lies after eight months of free fall, or not quite fourteen months from departure. We're only a couple of months from the critical moment right now. If we start back at once, we'll still have been gone from Earth for about 76 years. Each day we wait adds months to the return trip. No wonder there's impatience!'

'I see,' she said. 'What they're afraid of, the ones who want to go back, is that the Earth they knew will have slipped away from them, changed beyond recognition, in the extra time. But can't they understand that it already has?'

'Maybe they're afraid to understand,' Coffin said.

'You keep surprising me, Captain,' said Teresa with a hint of her smile. 'You actually show a bit of human sympathy.'

And, thought a far-off impersonal part of Coffin, *you showed enough to put me at ease by getting me to lecture you with safe impersonal figures*. But he didn't mind. She had succeeded. He could now free-sit, face to face, alone, and talk to her like a friend.

'What puzzles me,' he said, 'is why anybody at all, not to speak of so many, wants to give up. If we turned home this minute, we'd only save about seven years. Why don't we simply continue to Rustum and decide there what to do?'

'I think that's impossible,' said Teresa. 'You see, no one in his right mind wants to be a pioneer. To explore, yes; to settle rich new country with known and limited hazards, yes; but not to risk his children, his whole racial future, on as wild a gamble as this. The colonizing project resulted from an insoluble conflict at home. If that conflict has ended —'

'But ... you and Lochaber ... you pointed out that it has not ended. That at best, Earth offers you a breathing spell.'

'Still, most people would like to believe otherwise, wouldn't they?'

'All right,' said Coffin. 'But I'm sure a number of people now in deepsleep would agree with you and elect to stay on Rustum. Why can't we take them there first? It seems only fair. Then those who don't want to settle can return with the fleet.'

'Uh-uh.' Her hair was short, but it floated in loose waves when she shook her head, and light rippled mahogany across it. 'I've studied your reports. A handful couldn't survive on Rustum. Three thousand is none too many. It will have to be unanimous, whatever is decided.'

'I was trying to avoid that conclusion,' he said wearily, 'but I guess I can't. Okay, why don't they want to look Rustum over and put it to a vote? The quitters must realize they have a majority. They can afford to do the fair thing.'

'No. And I'll tell you why, Captain,' she said. 'I know Coenrad de Smet well, and one or two others. They're good men. You do wrong to call them quitters. But they do believe, quite honestly, it's best to go back. Now maybe they haven't figured it out consciously, but they must know intuitively that if we got to Rustum, the vote might well go against them. I've seen plenty of your photographs, Captain. Rustum may be hard and dangerous, but it's so beautiful that I can hardly wait for the reality. There's room, freedom, unpoisoned air. We'll remember all that we hated on Earth; we'll see the horror of going back into deepsleep; we'll reflect much more soberly than now, when we're fed up with being in space, how long a time will have passed before we can get back to Earth, and what a gamble we'd be taking on finding a tolerable situation there. Except for the higher gravity, and it won't seem so bad until we start doing heavy manual labor, none of the hardships of Rustum will have touched us; whereas the hardships of space travel and of Earth will still be vivid memories. A lot of people will change their minds and vote to stay. Perhaps a majority will. De Smet knows that. He won't risk it. He might get trapped himself, by the glamor of Rustum!'

Coffin murmured thoughtfully: 'After just a few days of deceleration, there won't be enough reaction mass left to do anything but continue back to Sol.'

'De Smet knows that too,' said Teresa. 'Captain, you can make a hard decision and stick to it. That's why you have your job. But maybe you forget how few people can – how most of us pray that someone or something will come along and tell us what to do. Even under severe pressure, the decision to go to Rustum was difficult. Now that there's a chance to undo our act, to go back to being safe and comfortable – but nevertheless a real risk that by the time we get home, Earth will no longer be safe or comfortable for anyone – we've been forced to decide all over again. It's agony, Captain! De Smet and his supporters are strong men, in their way. They'll compel us to do the irrevocable, as soon as possible, simply because it will make a final commitment. Once we're really headed back, it'll be out of our hands. We can stop thinking.'

He regarded her with a sort of wonder. 'But you look calm enough,' he said.

'I made my decision back on Earth,' she said. 'I've seen no reason to change it.'

'What's the consensus of the women?' he asked, leaping back to safely denumerable things.

'Most want to give up, of course.' She said it with a mildness that softened the judgment. 'They came only because their men wanted to. Women are much too practical to care about a philosophy or a frontier, or anything except their families.'

'Do you?' he challenged.

She shrugged ruefully. 'I have no family, Captain. At the same time, I suppose ... a sense of humor? ... kept me from sublimating it into a Cause of any kind.' Counterattacking: 'Why do you care what we do?'

'Why?' He found himself stammering. 'Why ... be-be-because I'm in charge —'

'Oh, yes. But also, you spent years promoting the idea of a Rustum colony. And then you accepted this thankless job, commanding the colonial fleet, when you might have been off doing your real work, visiting some star men have never visited before. Rustum must be a deep symbol to you. Don't worry. I won't go analytic. I happen to think myself that this colony is enormously important. If our race muffs this chance, we may never get another. But that's only an academic proposition, really. Why does it matter so much to me, personally, unless it touches some intimate basic in me? Let's face the facts, Captain. Neither of us is a bit cold-blooded about this. We *need* to have that colony planted.'

She stopped, laughed, and color went across her cheeks. 'Oh, dear, I do chatter, don't I? Pardon me. Let's get back to business.'

'I think,' said Coffin, slowly and jaggedly, 'thanks to your remarks, I'm beginning to realize what's involved.'

She settled back and listened.

He bent a leg around a stanchion to hold his lean body in place and beat one fist softly into the palm of the other hand. 'Yes, God help us, it is an emotional issue,' he said, the words carving the idea to shape. 'Logic is entirely irrelevant. There are some who want so badly to go to Rustum and be free, or whatever they hope to be there, that they'll dice with their lives for the privilege – and their wives' and children's lives. Others went reluctantly, against their own survival instincts, and now that they think they see a way of retreat, something they can justify to themselves, they'll fight any man who tries to bar it. Yes. It's a ghastly situation. One way or another, the decision has got to be made soon. And the facts can't be hidden. Every deepsleeper must be wakened and nursed to health by someone now conscious. The word will pass, year after year, always to a different combination of spacemen and colonists. Whatever is done, a proportion of them will be furious at what was decided while they slept. No, furious is too weak a word. Onward or backward, whichever way we go, we've struck at the emotional roots of people. And interstellar space can break the calmest men.... How long before just the wrong percentage of malcontents, weaklings, and shaky sanities goes on duty? What's going to happen then? Lord God of Hosts, deliver us or we perish!'

He sucked in an uneven breath. 'I'm sorry,' he faltered. 'I shouldn't—'

'Blow off steam? Why not?' she asked calmly. 'Would it be better to keep on being the iron man, till one day you put a pistol to your head?'

'You see,' he said in his misery, 'I'm *responsible*. Men and women – children— But I'll be in deepsleep. I'd go crazy if I tried to stay awake the whole voyage; the organism can't take it. I'll be asleep, and there'll be nothing I can do, but these ships were given into my care!'

He began to shiver. She took both his hands. Neither of them spoke for a long while.

4

When he left the *Pioneer* Coffin felt oddly hollow, as if he had opened his chest and pulled out heart and lungs. But his mind functioned with machine precision. For that he was grateful to Teresa. She had helped him discover what the facts were. It was a brutal knowledge, but without such understanding the expedition might well be doomed.

Or might it? Dispassionately, now, Coffin estimated chances. Either they went on to Rustum or they turned back. In either case, while the likelihood of survival could not be gauged in percentages, the odds would be poor. Better than fifty-fifty, no doubt, but not a hazard that the captain had any right to take, if he could avoid it by any means.

But what means were there?

As he hauled himself toward the *Ranger*, Coffin watched the receiver web grow in his eyes till it snared a distorted Milky Way. It seemed very frail to have carried so much hell. And, indeed, it would have to be dismantled before deceleration. No trick to sabotage the thing. But too late for that. *If only I had known!*

Or if someone on Earth, the villain or well-meaning fool or whatever he was who wrote that first message ... if only he would send another. 'Ignore preceding. Educational decree still in force.' Or something. But no. Such things didn't happen. A man had to make his own luck.

Coffin sighed and clamped bootsoles to his flagship's airlock.

Mardikian helped him through. When he removed his hoarfrosted space helmet, Coffin saw how the boy's mouth quivered. A few hours had put years on Mardikian.

He was in medical whites. Unnecessarily, to break the silence with any inane remark, Coffin said: 'Going on vat duty, I see.'

'Yes, sir.' A mutter. 'My turn.' The armor made a lot of noise while they stowed it. 'We'll need some more ethanol soon, Captain,' blurted Mardikian in a desperate voice.

'What for?' grumbled Coffin. He had often wished the stuff were not indispensable. He alone had the key to its barrel. Some masters allowed a small liquor ration on voyages, and said Coffin was only disguising prejudice in claiming it added risk. ('What the devil can happen in interstellar orbit? The only reason anyone stays conscious is, the machinery to care properly for sleepers would mass more than the extra supplies do. You can issue the grog when a man comes off watch, can't you? Oh, never mind, never mind, you damned bluenose! I'm just grateful I don't ship under you.')

'Gammagen fixative ... and so on ... sir,' stumbled Mardikian. 'Mr. Hallmyer will ... make the requisition as usual.'

'Okay.' Coffin faced his radio man, captured the fearful eyes, and snapped, 'I don't suppose there have been any further communications?'

'From Earth? No. No, sir. I ... I wouldn't really expect it ... we're about at the, the, the limit of reception now. ... It's almost a miracle, sir, I believe, that we picked up the first. Of course, we barely might get another—' Mardikian's words trailed off.

Coffin continued to stare. At last: 'They've been giving you a hard time, haven't they?'

'What?'

'The ones like Lochaber, who want to go on. They wish you'd had the sense to keep your mouth shut, at least till you consulted me. And then others, like de Smet, have said the opposite. Even over telecircuit, it's no fun being a storm center, is it?'

'No, sir. ...'

Coffin turned away. Why torment the fellow more? This thing had happened, that was all. And the fewer who realized the danger, and were thereby put under still greater stress, the less that danger would be.

'Avoid such disputes,' ordered Coffin. 'Most especially, don't brood over those which do arise. That's just begging for a nervous breakdown – out here. Carry on.'

Mardikian gulped and went aft.

Coffin drifted athwartships. The vessel thrummed around him.

He was not on watch, and had no desire to share the bridge with whoever was. He should eat something, but the idea was nauseating; he should try to sleep, but that would be useless. How long had he been with Teresa, while she cleared his mind and gave him what comfort she had to offer? A couple of hours. In fourteen hours or less, he must confront the spokesmen of crew and colonists. And meanwhile the fleet seethed.

On Earth, he thought wearily, a choice between going on and turning back would not have drawn men so close to insanity, even if the time elements had been the same. But Earth was long domesticated. Maybe, centuries ago, when a few wind-powered hulks wallowed forth upon hugeness, unsure whether they might sail off the world's edge, there had been comparable dilemmas. Yes, hadn't Columbus' men come near mutiny? Even unknown, though, and monster-peopled by superstition, Earth had not been as cruel an environment as space; nor had a caravel been as unnatural as a spaceship. Medics for hundreds of years had known how quickly a loss of external stimuli brought on hallucinations – and a cramped, sterile, vacuum-enclosed spaceship, month after month after month, began to affect the human mind rather like bandaged vision when afloat in a tank of warm water. Minds could never have disintegrated as quickly in midocean (sun and moon, wind and rain, the infinite shifting pattern of waves, the hope of catching a fish or seeing an island) as they did between the stars. It was accepted that a spaceman near the end of his year-watch was not quite sane.

If a mind so shaky were given a perfectly genuine wrong to brood on —

Coffin grew aware, startled, that he had wandered to the

radio shack.

He entered. It was a mere cubbyhole, one wall occupied by gleaming electronic controls, the rest full of racked equipment, tools, testers, spare parts, half-assembled units for this and that special purpose. The fleet did not absolutely need a Com officer – any spaceman could do the minimal jobs, and any officer had intensive electronics training – but Mardikian was a good, conscientious, useful technician.

His trouble was, perhaps, only that he was human.

Coffin pulled himself to the main receiver. A tape whirred slowly between spools, preserving what the web gathered. Coffin looked at a clipboard. Mardikian had written half an hour ago: 'Nothing received. Tape wiped and reset, 1530 hr.' Maybe since then —? Coffin flipped a switch. A scanner went quickly through the recording, found only cosmic noise – none of the orderliness which would have meant code or speech – and informed the man.

Now if it had just —

Coffin grew rigid. He floated among the mechanisms for a long time, blank-eyed as they. Alone the quick harsh breath showed him to be alive.

O God, help me do that which is right.

But what is right?

I should wrestle with Thine angel until I knew. But there is no time. Lord, be not wroth with me because I have no time.

Anguish ebbed. Coffin got busy.

Decision would be reached at the meeting, fourteen hours hence. A message which was to affect that decision must be received before then. But not very much before; nor very late, eleventh-hour reprieve style, either.

What should its wording be? Coffin didn't have to look up the previous one. It was branded on his brain. An invitation to return and talk matters over. But necessarily short, compact, with minimum redundancy: which meant an increased danger of misinterpretation.

He braced himself before the typer and began to compose, struck out his words and started again, and again and again. It had to be exactly right. A mere cancellation of the first message wouldn't do. Too pat. And a suspicion, turned over and over in the mind during a year watch, could be as destructive of sanity as could an outright sense of betrayal. So ...

Since fleet now approaching equal-time point, quick action necessary. Colonization plans abandoned. Expedition ordered, repeat ordered to return to Earth. Education decree already rescinded (a man back home wouldn't be certain the first beam had made contact) *and appeals for further concessions will be permitted through proper channels. Constitutionalists reminded that their first duty is to put their skills at disposal of society.*

Would that serve? Coffin read it over. It didn't contradict the first one; it only changed a suggestion to a command, as if someone were growing more frantic by the hour. (And a picture of near-chaos in government wasn't attractive, was it?) The bit about 'proper channels' underlined that speech was not free on Earth, and that the bureaucracy could restore the school decree whenever it wished. The pompous last sentence ought to irritate men who had turned their backs on the thing which Terrestrial society was becoming.

Maybe it could be improved, though. ... Coffin resumed work.

When he ripped out his last version, he was astonished to note that two hours had passed. Already? The ship seemed very quiet. Too quiet. He grew feverishly aware that anyone might break in on him at any time.

The tape could run for a day, but was usually checked and wiped every six or eight hours. Coffin decided to put his words on it at a spot corresponding to seven hours hence. Mardikian would have come off vat duty, but probably be asleep; he wouldn't play back until shortly before the council meeting.

Coffin turned to an auxiliary recorder. He had to tape his voice through a circuit which would alter it beyond recognition. And, of course, the whole thing had to be blurred, had to fade and come back, and to be full of squeals and buzzes and the crackling talk of the stars. No easy job to blend so many elements, in null-gee at that. Coffin lost himself in the task. He dared not do otherwise, for then he would be alone with himself.

Plug in this modulator, add an oscillation – let's see, where's that slide rule, what quantities do you want for —

'What are you doing?'

Coffin twisted about. Fingers clamped on his heart.

Mardikian floated in the doorway, looking dazed and afraid as he saw who the intruder was. 'What's wrong, sir?' he asked.

'You're on watch,' breathed Coffin. 'Vat duty.'

'Tea break, sir. I thought I'd check and —' The boy pushed himself into the shack. Coffin saw him framed in meters and transformer banks, like some futuristic saint. But sweat glistened on the dark young face, broke free and drifted in tiny spheroids toward the ventilator grille.

'Get out of here,' said Coffin thickly. And then: 'No! I don't mean that. Stay where you are!'

'But —' Almost, the captain could read a mind: *If the old man has gone space dizzy, name of fate, what's to become of us?* 'Yes, sir.'

Coffin licked sandy lips. 'Everything's okay,' he said. 'You surprised me, our nerves are on edge. That's why I hollered.'

'S-s-sorry, sir.'

'Anyone else around?'

'No, sir. All on duty or —' *I shouldn't have told him that!* Coffin read. *Now he knows I'm alone with him.*

'Everything's okay, son,' repeated the captain. But his voice came out like a buzz saw cutting through bone. 'I had a little project here I was, uh, playing with, and – uh —'

'Yes, sir. Of course.' *Humor him till I can get away. Then see Mr. Kivi. Let him take the responsibility. I don't want it! I don't want to be the skipper-in-chief, with nobody between me and the sky. It's too much. It'll crack a man wide open.*

71

Mardikian's trapped eyes circled the room. They fell on the typer, and the drafts Coffin had not yet destroyed.

Silence closed in.

'Well,' said Coffin at last. 'Now you know.'

'Yes, sir.' Mardikian could scarcely be heard.

'I'm going to fake this onto the receiver tape.'

'B-b — Yes, sir.' *Humor him!* Mardikian's nostrils flared with terror.

'You see,' rasped Coffin, 'it has to look genuine. This ought to get their backs up. They'll be more united on colonizing Rustum than they ever were before. As for me, though, I'll resist them. I'll claim I have my orders to turn about and don't want to get into trouble. Finally, of course, I'll let myself be talked into continuing, however reluctantly. So nobody will suspect me of ... fraud.'

Mardikian's lips moved soundlessly. He was close to hysteria, Coffin saw.

'It's unavoidable,' the captain said, and cursed himself for the roughness in his tone. Though maybe no orator could persuade this boy. What did he know of psychic breaking stress, who had never been tried to his own limit? 'We'll have to keep the secret, you and I, or —' No, what was the use? Within Mardikian's short experience, it was so much more natural to believe that one man, Coffin, had gone awry, than to understand a month-by-month rotting of the human soul under loneliness and frustration.

'Yes, sir,' Mardikian husked. 'Of course, sir.'

Even if he meant that, Coffin thought, *he might talk in his sleep. Or I might; but the admiral, alone of the whole fleet, has a completely private room.*

He racked his tools, most carefully, and faced about. Mardikian shoved away, bulging-eyed. 'No,' whispered Mardikian. 'No. Please.'

He opened his mouth to scream, but he didn't get time. Coffin chopped him on the neck. As he doubled up, Coffin gripped him with legs and one hand, balled the other fist, and hit him often in the solar plexus.

Mardikian rolled in the air like a drowned man.

Swiftly, then, Coffin towed him down the corridor to the pharmacy room. He unlocked the alcohol barrel, tapped a hypo, diluted it with sufficient water, and injected. Lucky the fleet didn't carry a real psychiatrist. If you broke, you went into deepsleep and weren't revived till you got home again to the clinics.

Coffin dragged the boy to a point near the airlock and shouted. Hallmyer came from the bridge. 'He started raving and attacked me,' panted the captain. 'I had to knock him out.'

Mardikian was roused for a checkup, but since he only mumbled incoherently, he was given a sedative. Two men began processing him for the vat. Coffin said he would make sure the Com officer hadn't damaged any equipment. He went back to the radio shack.

5

Teresa Zeleny met him. She did not speak, but led him to her room.

'Well,' he said, strangling on it, 'so we're continuing to Rustum, by unanimous vote. Aren't you happy?'

'I was,' she said quietly, 'till now, when I see that you aren't. I doubt if you're worried about legal trouble on Earth. You have authority to ignore such orders if the situation warrants. So what is the matter?'

He stared beyond her. 'I shouldn't have come here,' he said. 'But I had to talk with someone, and only you might understand. Will you bear with me a few minutes? I won't bother you again.'

'Not till Rustum.' Her smile was a gesture of compassion. 'And it's no bother.' After waiting a bit: 'What did you want to say?'

He told her, in short savage words.

She grew a little pale. 'The kid was actually dead drunk, and they didn't know it when they processed him?' she said. 'That's a grave risk. He might die.'

'I know,' said Coffin, and covered his eyes.

Her hand fell on his shoulder, 'I suppose you've done the only possible thing,' she said with much gentleness. 'Or, if there was a better way, you didn't have time to think of it.'

He said through his fingers, while his head turned away from her: 'If you don't tell on me, and I know you won't, then you're violating your own principles too: total information, free discussion and decision. Aren't you?'

She sighed. 'I imagine so. But doesn't every principle have its limits? How libertarian, or kind ... how human can you be, out here?'

'I shouldn't have told you.'

'I'm glad you did.'

Then, briskly, as if she too fled something, the woman said: 'If, as we both hope, Mardikian lives, then the truth is bound to come out when your fleet returns to Earth. So we'll need to work out a defense for you. Or can you plead necessity?'

'It doesn't matter.' He raised his head, and now he could speak steadily. 'I don't figure to skulk more than I must. Let them say what they will, eight decades hence. I'll already have been judged.'

'What?' She retreated a pace, perhaps to see the gaunt form better. 'You don't mean you'll stay on Rustum? But that isn't necessary! We can —'

'A liar ... quite likely a murderer ... I am not worthy to be the master of a ship.' His tone cracked over. 'And maybe, after all, there isn't going to be any more space travel to come home to.'

He jerked free of her and went through the door. She stared after him. She had better let him out; no, the key had been left in the bulkhead lock. She had no excuse to follow.

You aren't alone, Joshua, she wanted to call. *Every one of us is beside you. Time is the bridge that always burns behind us.*

1

In itself, the accident was ridiculous. The damage could have been repaired in a week or so. There would have been no permanent harm to anything except pride.

But because it happened where it did, Fleet Captain Nils Kivi took one look at his instruments and read death.

'*Jesu Kristi!*' Vibrations of impact and shearing still toned in the metal around him. Weightlessness, as the ion blast died, was like being pitched off a cliff. He heard a wail as air escaped, then a clash as the pierced section was automatically closed off. None of it registered. His entire self was speared on the needle of the radiation meter.

A second he hung there. His mind returned to him. He grabbed a stanchion and yanked himself to the control console. His finger pushed the intercom button. He said, 'Abandon ship!' in a gasp that was amplified to a roar.

The drill had not been carried out for a long time, but his body drowned panic in adrenalin and he went through efficient motions. One hand slipped free the spool of data tape from the autopilot and stuck it in a pocket of his coverall. (He even recollected reading somewhere that the captain of a foundering ocean vessel on Earth, long ago, had always taken the log with him.) His foot shoved vigorously against a recoil chair, sent him arrowing toward the bridge door with a slight spin which he corrected by slapping a wall. Once out in the corridor, he pulled himself hand over hand until the rungs he grasped at seemed blurred with his speed.

Others joined him from their posts of duty, a dozen men with faces hardened against fear. Some had already entered the ferry, which was now to be a lifeboat. Kivi could hear its generators whine, building up potentials. He hung aside to let his men stream through the linked airlocks. Engineer Abdul Barang was last. Kivi followed him in, asking: 'Do you know what happened? Something seems to have knocked out the atomics.'

'A heavy object. Ripped through the deck from the after hold, into the engine room, and out the side.' Barang looked savage. 'Loose cargo, I'm certain.'

'The colonist—'

'Svoboda? I don't know. Are we waiting for him? He might have killed us.'

Kivi nodded. 'Strap in,' he called, unnecessarily, for the men were finding their places. Barang sped aft to take over the power plant from whoever had had the presence of mind to start it going. Kivi went to the pilot board at the head of the passenger section. His fingers flew, adjusting his harness. Each instant he delayed, death sleeted through his body. 'Call off,' he said, heard the names and knew the tally was full. He got settled and punched the airlock controls. The boat valve started to close.

A final man burst through. He screamed in English: 'Were you going to leave me there?'

Kivi, who understood him, replied coldly: 'Why not? You might have been dead for all we knew, or had time to discover. And you're responsible for this.'

'What?' Jan Svoboda floated in the aisle like an ungainly, wildly gesturing fish. The eyes of men raked him from the seats. '*I'm* responsible?' he choked. 'Why, you self-righteous jackass, you personally agreed that—'

Kivi hit the launching button. The ship released the ferry. Repulsors boosted the smaller hull free of the larger. Kivi didn't stop to take sights. Any direction is the best way out when you are in the middle of hell. He simply crammed down the emergency manual lever. The boat rumbled and leaped. Svoboda was thrown back by the acceleration. He hit the after bulkhead of the passenger section hard enough to crack its plastic. There he lay, pinned down, his face one mask of blood. Kivi wondered if his neck was broken. Almost, if not quite, the captain hoped so.

2

Men finding places for themselves on the *Courier* made her passageways buzz with their unease. Pulling himself along toward sickbay, Kivi threw out a bow wave of silence. Bad enough to be any master, losing any ship. But since old Coffin had so inexplicably resigned to join the settlers, Nils Kivi was in command of the entire fleet. The vessel lost was the *Ranger*, flagship of the other fourteen. The spacemen could do without her, since the disembarkation of the passengers had left ample room. But almost forty-one years of voyaging lay ahead of them, from e Eridani back to Sol. Anything might become an obsession during a year-watch, destroying minds, even destroying men. Surely an admiral who lost his flagship was a dark symbol.

Angrily, Kivi suppressed his own thoughts. He was a short, stocky man, with the high cheekbones and slightly oblique blue eyes of the Ladogan. Normally he was cheerful, talkative, a bit of a dandy. But at the moment he was going to see Jan Svoboda.

He stopped at a certain one of the ship's flimsy interior doors, opened it and went through into a cubbyhole that combined anteroom and the medic's desk space. Another person was just emerging from the sickbay cabin beyond. They bumped together and cartwheeled aside. For an instant, Kivi hung staring. When words came, they were idiotic: 'But you are down on Rustum.'

Judith Svoboda shook her head. Loosened by the collision, her hair made a brown cloud about face and shoulders, with red gleams where it caught the light. She wore a plain coverall whose bagginess in zero gravity did not entirely hide a trim figure. 'I heard about the accident, and that Jan was hurt,' she said. 'The last ferry unloading the *Migrant* carried the word. Of course I hitched a ride upstairs again.'

He had always liked women's voices to be low, as hers was. Not that a spaceman saw many women. He roughened his own tones: 'Who's the pilot? You made him violate four separate regulations.'

'Have a heart,' she pleaded. Though English was still important enough in space that Kivi's fluency paid off, he was momentarily puzzled by the idiom. 'Jan is my husband,' she said. 'What else could I do but come to him?'

'Well.' Kivi stared at a microfile of medical references. 'Well. So you have just now seen him? How is he?'

'Better than I feared. He can get up soon — Up! Down!' she said bitterly. 'What does that mean in orbit?' With haste: 'Why did you take off so fast, Nils? Jan said you gave him no time to strap in.'

He sighed with a sudden weariness. 'Are you, too, about to heap fire on me for that? Your husband said enough nasty things about my action when he first regained consciousness. Spare me.'

'Jan's been under a great strain,' she said. 'And then to be so shocked and hurt.... Please don't blame him if he's intemperate.'

Kivi jerked his head around, startled, to look at her. 'Do you not accuse me?'

'I'm sure you had a good reason.' Her smile was lopsided. 'I just wondered what it might have been.'

Kivi harked back to the days and the nights down on Rustum. He had come to know her, while spacemen and colonists worked together; he had seen her smeared with grease, wrench in hand, helping assemble a tractor, and he had seen her beneath green leaves and by the cold hurtling light of the moon Sohrab. Yes, he thought, she would give any man a chance to explain. Even a spaceman.

Heavily, he said: 'We were in a radiation belt. We had no time to spare, not a second.'

'Was the radiation that intense? Really?'

'Perhaps I was hasty.' He must push those words out. Looking back, he could not give a full logical defense, in terms of the instrumented data, for having acted so fast that he might have abandoned Svoboda, or killed him in the blastoff. At the time, he had known only a whirl of hatred for the one who had wrecked his ship. And yet Svoboda was the husband of Judith and the father of her children.

It boiled up again within the captain. 'After all,' he snapped, 'had it not been for his carelessness, the situation would never have arisen.'

The heartshaped face before him grew tense. 'Is he actually responsible?' Judith asked, her tone becoming hostile. 'He says you gave him permission to work on the cargo.'

Kivi felt himself redden. 'I did. But I had no idea he meant to unsling a piece as massive as —'

'You could have asked him exactly what he intended to do. How was he to know it could be dangerous?'

'I assumed he had a normal amount of common sense. My mistake!'

A while they glared at each other. The cubicle grew very still. It was almost as if Kivi could sense the hollowness of the ship around him, empty holds, empty tanks, the vessel was a shell chained in orbit about Rustum. *So am I*, he thought. Then he remembered the nights down in High America, when campfires leaped to tint this woman's face against a great rustling darkness. Once he and she had been alone for a few hours, walking along the Emperor River in search of a wild orchard he had found on the first expedition, some ninety years ago. It hadn't been a notable adventure, only sunlight, bright water flowing beside them, glimpsed birds and animals. They hadn't even talked much. But he could not forget that day.

'I'm sorry,' said the captain. 'Doubtless he and I were both at fault.'

'Thanks.' Judith caught his hand between her own.

Presently she asked: 'What did happen? I'm so confused. The ferry pilot said one thing, Jan said another, and they speak about poison belts and none of it makes much sense to me. Do you even know yourself what the truth is?'

'I believe so. I'll have to inspect the derelict, but everything seems clear enough.' Kivi grimaced. 'Must I explain?'

'No. I wish you would, though.'

'Very well.'

When the fleet arrived at Rustum, it took up orbit around the planet, well beyond the Van Allen radiation zones and the primary meteorite hazard. Huge, frail, and ion-driven, the interstellar ships could never land. First crew, then colonists were roused and taken to High America in the ferries – rugged boats with retractible wings, propelled by thermal rather than electric jets. Since cargo discharge would be a slower process, the ships were one by one brought down into low orbit, scarcely above the planet's atmosphere, where they could be unloaded with more speed and convenience. This job engaged a certain proportion of their crews; other spacemen were on Rustum refining reaction mass for the homeward journey; the remainder – a majority – were told off to help the colonists with the labor of establishing a settlement.

But a few colonists must also be assigned to help in space. Much of the cargo was unfamiliar to astronauts: mining, agricultural, chemical equipment. Mass ratios were too high to allow conventional crating and padding. The stuff must be transferred to the ferries piece by piece, under knowledgeable supervision. Otherwise something thermoplastic might get stowed next to a heat shield, or a set of crystal standards get irradiated and ruined, or ... There weren't going to be any replacement parts from Earth.

As an engineer, Jan Svoboda was appointed one such cargomaster. When the *Ranger* started from high orbit to low, he requested permission to begin preparing the material for discharge, even during deceleration. As anxious as he to finish a miserable task, Kivi agreed.

The *Ranger* swung herself on gyros so the ion blast opposed her orbit. Thus checked, she spiraled inward at a safe, easy pace. She was in a nearly equatorial plane so that the ferries could take full advantage of the planet's rotation. The spiral therefore took her through the densest sections of the poison belts.

Like any world with a magnetic field, Rustum was surrounded by high-energy-charged particles which formed bands at various distances from its center. Even through safety screens maintained at full strength, Kivi noticed an increase in the radiation count. Nothing to worry about, of course —

Until the detectors registered a meteorite approaching along a possible collision path.

The few seconds of five-gravity blast by which the autopilot got the *Ranger* out of the way should have been routine. A warning whistle blew. Every man had ample time to lie down flat and grab hold of something solid. Rocks big enough to be worth dodging aren't exactly common, but neither are they so rare in planetary neighborhoods that the maneuver is news.

This time, however, Jan Svoboda had taken the slings off an object massing over one ton, part of a nuclear generator. He had wanted to gain access for purpose of disassembly. Only a light aluminum framework supported the thing. At five gravities, it tore loose. It went through the thin after deck, caromed off the fire chamber shielding, and smashed a hole in the engine room wall through which stars peered.

No one was hurt. The damage was not extreme. But it did involve a good deal of equipment auxiliary to the thermonuclear power plant. Designed to fail safe, the fusion reaction blinked out. Batteries took over, but they could only maintain the internal electrical system: not the ion drive or the radiation screen.

Suddenly the ship was full of roentgens.

The ferry had no room for antiradiation apparatus. It could only be used to escape before the crew got a serious dose. The *Ranger* drifted in orbit, abandoned. Invisible and inaudible, the poison currents seethed through her hull.

'I see.' Judith nodded. A rippling went along her hair. 'Thanks.'

Kivi's mouth seemed more dry than a few moments' talking warranted. 'Happy to oblige,' he mumbled.

'What are your plans now?'

'I—' Kivi's lips pressed together. 'Nothing. Never mind.'

'Did you come to see how Jan is? I was about to go arrange shipboard accommodations for myself till I can get another ferry back. I'm sure Jan would be glad if you—' Her voice trailed off. Svoboda had been curt enough with the captain, when they were all working down at camp.

Kivi put on an acid smile. 'To be sure.'

Inwardly he realized, with a jolt, that he didn't know why he had come here. To take out his own despair by railing at the injured man? He was afraid there had been some such idea in him, not far below the surface of consciousness. But why? Svoboda was moody, short-tempered, short-spoken; but not really more irritating than any other of his ground-grubbing fellows. As a Constitutionalist leader he had helped bring this colonizing project about – and surely no spaceman wanted the wretched assignment – yet a job was a job, to be completed rather than cursed.

'I ... yes, I wanted to see how he was,' blurted Kivi. 'And, and confer with him—'

'Well, you can now!'

Kivi twisted himself around the stanchion he gripped, to face the inner door. It stood open. Jan Svoboda hovered there.

He was in hospital pajamas, his features almost hidden by bandages; tape swathed his chest; the framework of an action splint was spidery around his broken left collarbone, to give him some use of that arm. 'Jan!' exclaimed Judith. 'Get back to bed!'

Svoboda grunted. 'What's a bed in free fall, except a harness to keep the air from blowing you away? I heard you talking.' His eyes stabbed past his white mask, toward the captain. 'Okay, here I am. Say what you want to say.'

'The medic—' protested Kivi.

'I'm not under his orders,' said Svoboda. 'I know how much I'm able to move around.'

'Jan,' said his wife. 'Please.'

'How polite am I supposed to be to a man who tried to murder me?'

'That will do!' rapped Kivi.

He could imagine the mouth sarcastically bending upward behind that cloth. 'Go on,' said Svoboda. 'I'm in no shape to fight. Or you can simply have me arrested, you being the captain. Go on, do whatever you came to do.'

Judith grew quite pale. 'Stop that, Jan,' she said. 'It's not fair to call a man a coward if he doesn't attack you, and a bully if he does.'

Silence came again. A minute had passed before Kivi realized he was staring at her.

Finally, rigidly, Svoboda said: 'All right. Conceded. I suppose we can talk about a practical problem without tantrums. Can that ship be recovered?'

Kivi pulled his eyes from Judith. 'I do not believe so,' he answered.

'Well, then, when can we start unloading her? I can still supervise that, though I may need an assistant.'

'Unload?' Kivi trudged back from other thoughts. 'What do you mean? The *Ranger* is in a poison belt. She can't be unloaded.'

'But wait a minute!' Svoboda grabbed the doorframe. His knuckles whitened. 'She's carrying stuff the colony has to have.'

'The colony must do without,' said Kivi. Anger returned to him, cold and flat.

'What? Do you — No, that's impossible! There must be a way to get those materials out of the ship.'

Kivi shrugged. 'We'll make an inspection, of course. But I see very little hope. Believe me, Svoboda, it is just as serious for me to lose the *Ranger* as for you to lose her cargo.'

Svoboda's masked head shook violently. 'Oh, no, it isn't. We have to stay on Rustum for the rest of our lives. Lacking some of that equipment, the lives will be short. You're going back to Earth.'

'Earth is a long way off,' said Kivi.

3

The *Migrant* eased in on the barest whisper of jets. Svoboda felt the bridge deck thrum faintly beneath his shoes. The existence of an 'under,' however small his weight, seemed a marvel.

Kivi looked up from his seat at the control console. 'There she is,' he said. 'Have a look while I bring us alongside.'

'What acceleration are you going to use?' asked Svoboda sharply.

Kivi's laugh barked at him. 'No more than half a gee. You needn't strap in.' He gave his attention back to the ship, tapping switches, speaking commands on the intercom. The vast bulk of the *Migrant* was guided primarily by the autopilot, even in maneuvers as close as this. Kivi's job amounted to telling the robot: 'Go toward yonder object.'

Suppressing a retort, Svoboda bent over the viewscreen. At top magnification, the *Ranger* seemed almost a toy; but she grew rapidly to his sight. The hull spun end for end, wobbling along the invariable plane. Shadows and harsh sunlight chased each other across the ugly awkward shape. Not for the first time, he thought that even the streamlined ferries were unhandsome. God, to stand on Rustum again and see the last ferry go skyward!

As for the alleged magnificence of space itself, he found the scene overrated. The stars were quite a sight, true, cold unblinking sparks through a clear darkness. But undimmed by atmosphere, there were too many of them. Only a professional could distinguish constellations in that unmeaningful swarm. And now, two-thirds of an Astronomical Unit distant, e Eridani had changed from star to sun. You had to look away from it to see anything except fire.

Kivi's voice jarred Svoboda aware again: 'Have you spotted the piece of equipment which did the damage? It ought to be in orbit near the ship.'

'No, not yet. It's probably wrecked anyway.' Svoboda squinted into the screen. Damn the undiffused illumination of airlessness! The view was a mere jumble of nights and highlights. 'I hope some of it can be salvaged, though. Then, once we get our machine shop set up at camp, the entire unit can be repaired.'

'I fear you are too optimistic. That stuff is gone forever.'

Svoboda turned to the other man. He had not quite appreciated the implications of Kivi's pessimism before this moment. Perhaps he hadn't dared think out what the captain meant. Now he knew horror. He could only say, feebly, 'Don't be ridiculous. Why can't we transfer the lading to this ship? For that matter, why can't we fix the *Ranger*?'

'Because the planet's magnetic field concentrates energetic charged particles in layers, and the *Ranger* happens to be in orbit at a mean distance of 11,600 kilometers from the center of Rustum, which happens to be the very middle of the inmost radiation zone,' said Kivi with elaborate sarcasm. 'Any person working on her would get a lethal dose in less than two days.'

'For God's sake!' exploded Svoboda. He raised his left arm. A jag of pain went along the broken, metal-splinted clavicle. 'Give me a straight answer! Our radiation screen extends outward for several kilometers from the hull. Why can't we lay alongside, enveloping the *Ranger* in the field?'

'Look,' said Kivi. Svoboda wasn't sure whether he was talking with strained patience or in continued mockery. 'I trust you know how a radiation screen works. The generator uses a magnetohydrodynamic principle to catch hold of charged particles and deflect them from the hull. But the particles in a Van Allen belt are extremely energetic. They are not easily deflected. Most of them penetrate far into the field – whose intensity obeys an approximate inverse square law – before their paths acquire an appreciable curvature. Therefore, the concentration of undeflected particles increases sharply with each meter you go beyond our hull.

'If we lay directly alongside the *Ranger*, a man who went aboard would be in a four-day lethal concentration at her central axis. I mean by that, fifty percent of humankind would die of radiation sickness if exposed for four days to such a dosage. On the opposite side of the *Ranger*, he would be in a two-and-a-half-day lethal concentration! Now do you understand?'

'Well ... no,' said Svoboda. 'The men needn't work continuously. They can take a few hours at a time, no more. Can't they?'

'No.' Kivi shook his head, peered at the control board, and tapped a stud. 'Quite aside from the radiation, they could do nothing. Remember, the force screen is a pulsating magnetic field of great strength. It's so heterodyned that it does not operate within the hull it protects. But if the *Migrant*'s screen enveloped the derelict ... do you see? Nothing more complicated than a thermal cutting torch could function. Certainly nothing electronic, probably not many things electrical. Since the smashed gear is essentially electronic, how shall it be fixed, recalibrated, and tested? How shall the very tools to make the repairs be operated?'

Svoboda said desperately: 'Well, why can't we tow the *Ranger*? We need only get her into clear space, out of this zone. Then anyone can safely go aboard. How much orbital radius need we lose? Fifteen hundred kilometers? Two thousand?'

'We'd wreck another ship if we tried that,' snapped Kivi. 'One vessel cannot pull another. The ion blast would disintegrate the one being towed. As for pushing – the least unbalance, and they'd collide and crumple.'

'We could weld them together with girders. Maybe attach one ship to each side of the derelict.'

'You have exaggerated ideas. At nine-to-one mass ratios, interstellar craft are not built like bulldozers. They have only moderate strength against longitudinal forces, and very little against any lateral push. Playing tugboat, they would yank the ribs out of themselves. I thought of the idea too, you see, and did some calculation, so I have figures to prove it's impossible.'

'But the ferryboats —'

'Yes, the ferries are sturdier. Two of them could do the job. But there would have to be crewmen aboard. So jerry-built a system could not be controlled remotely. And what shall protect those men from the radiation? The ferries have no screen generators. If a spaceship paced the ferries so closely that its own field gave a little protection – enough protection, even, for a man to stay aboard ten minutes – then that field would bollix up the ferries' electronic system. So that's out, too. Now shut your mouth!'

Kivi concentrated on the approach maneuver as if it were his enemy. Svoboda sat in angry silence. Faintly he could hear the ship murmur around him, engines, oxygenators, airblowers, echoes down long resonant passageways. It was like being swallowed alive by some giant fish, he thought, and hearing its metabolism close in. He strangled on the wish to escape.

Only, he thought, vacuum lay outside, the sun was a blowtorch and shadows were colder than charity. Senses, untrained for free fall and shifting accelerations, had made his cargomaster job a prolonged martyrdom. Antinausea pills kept him functioning, most of the time, but took away his appetite; the weakness of ill-nourished days underlay the shock and blood loss lately suffered. If Kivi knew how hard it had been not to let go of every stretched nerve and scream aloud, Kivi would be less vicious. But Svoboda was damned if he would tell the Finn.

Suddenly he slumped with weariness. It was almost as if he could remember the journey hither, not only the grind-stone year when he stood watch, but the suspended anima-tion period itself, four decades in darkness. He hardly noticed the little bump of contact, nor the resumption of free fall, nor the quiver in the ship as grapnels made fast. He had unstrapped before the captain's words registered:

'— and don't touch anything while you wait. Understand?'

'Huh?' Svoboda gaped. 'Where are you going?'

'To put on a spacesuit and look over the wreck. Did you

think I was bound for a tiddlywink tournament?'

'But the radiation —'

'The *Migrant*'s field will screen me enough that I can stand an hour or two.'

'Well, wait, I'll come too. I want to check the cargo.'

'No, stay here. You've already gotten a hefty dose, when the accident happened.'

'So did you. Send a crewman who wasn't along at the time, rather than either of us.'

Kivi squared his shoulders. 'I am the captain,' he said, and left the bridge.

Svoboda made no move to follow. His exhaustion was still upon him. And he thought dully that, well, Kivi wasn't married. Few spacemen were. Whereas Judith had spoken about having more children. . . . Best not expose himself to any unnecessary radiation.

Why did I come on this trip at all, then? he wondered. *I could have stayed aboard the* Courier *with her – No. I have to make sure Kivi doesn't give up.*

It would be only too natural for the commander to abandon the cargo. Why take risks for the sake of some damned colonists? Svoboda remembered scene after scene down at camp, quarrels flaring between the settlers and the spacemen assigned to help them. Groundbreaking, tree felling, concrete pouring, well drilling, were not work for an astronaut. To make it still more of an insult, they must take orders from the despised clodhuggers. No wonder the most trivial friction could make a man lose control. So far there had been nothing worse than fist fights, but Svoboda felt sure Kivi shared his own nightmare: knives and guns drawn, the Emperor River turned red.

Surely, Svoboda thought, no rational motive drove men to make such voyages, again and again and again, returning each time to an Earth grown more alien by decades. The spacemen were explorers. Their mystique could not be reconciled with that of the Constitutionalists, who had dragged these ships to Rustum because of a preoccupation with details of government which the spacemen found ridiculous. *No wonder we don't get along with each other. The two parties belong to two different civilizations.*

His eyes went to the screen. Linked, derelict and ship formed a new object with its own angular momentum and inertial constants. The complex pattern of spin had changed, though still too slow to give any noticeable weight. Now the bridge turret faced Rustum.

The planet was near half phase. Its shield sprawled across 64 degrees of sky, a great vague circle whose dark half was rimmed in fire where atmosphere refracted sunlight and whose dayside was so brilliant that it drowned the stars. The edges were hazed, but Svoboda could see ghostly auroral banners shaken loose just above the night limb. The basic sunlit color was blue, shading from turquoise to opal. Clouds belted the planet with white, subtle red and gray tints. Beneath them, he could just make out a pair of continents, brownish green splotches. He thought of standing there, under a hard steady pull of gravitation, tasting wind. Rustum grew so beautiful to him that he gulped back tears.

He reminded himself that the surface was dense forest, chill desert, unclimbable scarps, hurricanes, rain, snow, and drought, a hostile ecology, poisonous plants, wild animals. Three thousand isolated humans would not survive without machines and scientific instruments.

Nonetheless he remained staring at it like a modernistic Lucifer. The rapid orbit of the ships, two hours and 43 minutes to complete a circuit, swung him dayward. Presently he was nearly blinded by sunlight, focused to a single point by a curving ocean surface. He squinted, seeking details. Yes, that continent was Roxana. The children were there —

'Still waiting?' said Kivi behind him.

Svoboda turned. In his tension he lost a handhold and drifted free of his seat. He kicked ignominiously in midair till Kivi pulled him back.

'Well?' His voice came out shrill.

'No use,' said Kivi. He looked away. 'We can do nothing.

The damage is too extensive for a jury rig. That ship is lost.'

'But for mercy's sake, man! I don't care about the damned ship. We have to get the cargo out. Do you want to kill us?'

'I do not want to kill my own men.' Kivi scowled at the thin foam of the Milky Way. 'What in that lading is so crucial?'

'Everything. An atomic power generator. Part of a synthesizing laboratory. Biometric apparatus —'

'Can't you get along without it?'

'Rustum isn't Earth! We can't eat many native life forms. Terrestrial plants won't grow without ecological and chemical preparation. There are probably diseases, or will be as soon as a few native viruses mutate, to which we've no racial immunity whatever. We can't dig and refine minerals at the rate we've got to have them without high-energy equipment, which requires a nuclear generator.'

'You can build what you need.'

'We can *not*. What'd we eat and wear and use for tools in the meantime? We took along a bare minimum of equipment as it is.' Svoboda shook his head. 'I've got a couple of kids, you know. I'm not about to risk their lives more than the original plan requires.'

Kivi sighed. 'Well, then, tell me how to recover any significant portion of that cargo. I'm listening.'

'Isn't it obvious? The force screen of this ship will give enough protection for a man to work a few hours, unloading by hand, transferring the stuff here. If every crewman will take, say, a four-hour trick, the job can be done.'

Kivi shook his head. 'I doubt it. I have better than 1600 men, yes. But transferring cargo without machinery, I think would take more than 1600 times four man-hours. Even if not, I can't order my men to do this. The cargo is not essential to our survival, you see. Radiation effects being cumulative, and a spaceman getting far more than is good for him even under the best of conditions, regulations do not allow me to order men into unnecessary exposure. I'd have to ask for volunteers. I wouldn't get any – for the sake of you groundgrubbers.'

Svoboda stared at Kivi. It was like a bad dream, he thought. They made noises at each other, but somehow meaning did not get across.

'All right,' he said. 'We'll transfer the cargo ourselves. We colonists.'

Kivi laughed aloud, with no merriment. 'Do you seriously believe so? Why, untrained men would take so long about it, the radiation would kill them before they had properly started!'

The captain looked closely at his passenger. Briefly, there was a mildening in those slant eyes. 'This is not easy for me either, you know,' he added quietly. 'Earth has fewer spaceships each generation. I have lost one. I would rather have lost both my hands.'

After a moment, he continued: 'Well, I suggest you flit downstairs and debate the matter with your friends. They can decide if they want to continue under the new circumstances. Those who don't can return home with the fleet. We can take them, distributed among the remaining ships, if we have larger watches to reduce the deepsleep apparatus needed.'

'But that will be all of us!' Svoboda cried. *'The few who are stubborn enough to remain will be too few to survive under any conditions. You have just sentenced the Rustum colony to death, and thereby everything the colony believed in. It's all been for nothing.'*

'I'm sorry,' said the Finn.

He whipped himself into the pilot chair and fastened his harness. 'Back to the *Courier*,' he said into the intercom. 'Stand by for casting loose of derelict and blastoff.'

His fingers paused above the board. 'There is one other thing, Svoboda,' he said. 'Even if my men did agree to unload for you, which I know they won't, I should not allow them to.'

Svoboda hunched together. He had taken too many blows. Starlight filled his eyes, but did not reach his consciousness. 'Why?' he said.

'Because the job would add weeks to our stay here,' answered Kivi. 'Only a few men at a time could be aboard the *Ranger*. The rest must stay cooped idle on the other ships, or on ground. Either alternative is explosive.'

'What?'

'It's one thing for an all-male expedition to visit a star.' Kivi's tones were thin. 'It's another to mingle with a thousand nubile women, none of them ours. What do you think the basic reason is for the enmity and fights you've witnessed? How long till such a fight ends in someone's death? And if that doesn't touch off a riot, I don't know what will. – And yet I can't force my men to sit in orbit, week after week, when they might be on ground. We have a long voyage ahead of us. I dare not begin it with their morale shattered.'

Svoboda fastened himself in, though the onset of acceleration was weak enough. For the first time, he began to see that Kivi also had a right to be unreasonable.

He stared ahead of him. The poison rain should have been visible, he thought. He should have heard it hissing against the magnetic screen. Unsensed death warded off by unsensed armor, no, his mind could understand but his instincts rebelled. All they wanted was for him to hold Judith and the children close against him, under a sky which merely threw thunderbolts.

Bemused, he tried to convince himself of physics. Just because you can't see electrons and protons going by, you must not call them unreal. You can watch their trail through a cloud chamber, their signature on a photographic plate.... Magnetic fields are quite as real. A powerful magnet will snatch a knife from your hand and cut you if you go too near its poles. Planetary magnetism will swing a needle to guide you home.

For that matter, who ever saw or heard or measured an emotion? And yet love, hate, fear had driven men out between the stars, where despair broke them. The gross matter of a man's body could pace in circles, worrying, till an unweighable thought stopped him in his tracks. If only a thought could stop a spaceship in its orbit with the same ease. But an idea was not a magnetic field.

Or was it?

Svoboda leaped from his chair. He banged his left arm against the headrest. Anguish went in a wave through him, crested by his yell. Kivi looked around. 'What's wrong?' he barked.

Fighting back tears, Svoboda said through the throbbing: 'I believe I have a way. I have a way—'

'Will it take long?' asked Kivi, not impressed.

'It, it, it might.'

'Then forget it.'

'But Judas in hell!' Svoboda felt his collarbone. The splint seemed intact. Pain receded like a tide, advancing and retreating once more. He chose a moment when his brain was clear to choke out: 'Will you listen to me? We can save the ship too!'

'And risk losing twenty men by murder and riot. No.' Kivi's face was held straight forward, expressionless. 'I told you, the tension between our parties is already dangerous. I hardly dare wait long enough to unload the remaining ships and fill our tanks. Then we must go! Not an extra day will I spend in this God-hated place.'

'But the ship – you said—'

'I know. It will hurt my reputation to come back minus a ship. I may lose my command. But I am not a fanatic, Svoboda. You are willing to sacrifice Judith's life to preserve that weird philosophy of yours. (And what is it, anyhow, but an assertion of your own immortal importance?) I am not willing to let men be hurt, perhaps die, that my record may look good. I am going to bring a whole crew home, if not a whole fleet. And if you settlers give up and come home with us – as I think you will – before heaven, I'll have done you a favor!' He turned blind blue eyes around and yelled: 'Get out! I do not want to hear your crazy plan! Get off the bridge and leave me alone!'

4

There was even less privacy on a spaceship than there had been on Earth. Svoboda and his wife finally stopped looking for a place to be by themselves. They were ordered out of too many sections by crewmen who obviously enjoyed the ordering. They returned to the forecastle and free-sat behind drawn curtains in the bunk space assigned them. From time to time, the rattle of fantan sticks on a magnetized table and the jabber of voices interrupted them.

He saw through the gloom of the cramped space that her eyes were red and dark-ringed. She was worn down as far as himself. His helplessness to aid her chewed in him.

'But didn't he even hear your idea?' she asked. 'I can't understand that.'

'Oh, yes,' sighed Svoboda. 'He blew a fuse and ordered me off the bridge, as I've told you. But by the time we'd returned here to the *Courier*, he had cooled enough to hear me out when I insisted he do so. I'd used the interim to make some rough calculations, so I proved to him that my scheme really would work.'

She still hadn't asked him what it was. But that was typical of her. Like most women, she kept her warmth for human things and left the abstractions to her husband. He often thought she had come to Rustum less for her beliefs than for him.

Puzzled, she asked, 'He rejected your plan anyhow?'

'Yes. He listened, agreed it was practical, but claimed it was not practicable. When I started to argue, he lost his temper again and stormed away.'

'It isn't like Nils at all,' she murmured.

Svoboda started. 'What're you doing on first-name terms with him?'

'Why, I thought you knew —' Judith paused. 'No, maybe not. You kept so busy down at camp, and you were so cold to him, to all the spacemen. I could never see why. He was very kind, both to me and the children. He and Davy were almost inseparable. He taught Davy the local woodcraft, the tricks and trails he had learned on the first expedition.' She rubbed her eyes. 'That's why I don't understand his attitude now.'

'Well, he is under a strain too,' Svoboda admitted grudgingly. 'Losing that ship was a hard blow.'

'Then he ought to be all the more anxious to recover it.'

'Uh-huh. But he's right in claiming that my idea, while simple and elegant' – Svoboda grinned lopsidedly – 'will take a considerable time. A few crewmen will be kept busy. The rest will have nothing to do, once the last bottoms have been unloaded and the mass tanks refilled. There is certainly a good chance Satan will find mischief for idle hands.'

'Can't they go into deepsleep? They have to anyway, for the trip home.'

'No, I'm afraid not. My scheme does involve some high-powered maneuvering, spurts of several gravities' acceleration. Once they've been reassembled, the coldvats will be too lightly built to stand that. And every ship will be needed for this job, if it isn't to drag on impossibly long. . . . No, most of the crew will have to wait on the ground. Kivi is right. It can lead to trouble. He doesn't feel the risk is worth the gain. I do.'

A darkness crossed her. 'I wonder. Already —' She broke off.

'What?' rapped Svoboda.

'Nothing.'

He caught her wrist so she winced. 'Tell me! I have a right to know.'

'Nothing, I said! A man made a pass at me . . . one of the spacemen . . . a few days ago at camp. Nothing happened, really. I yelled and Charlie Lochaber came running. The spaceman made off. There wasn't even a fight.'

Svoboda stiffened before he said, harshly, 'There had

better be two separate camps. No social contact between them, and no colonist ever to be alone.'

'But that's horrible. Those men have worked hard for us. They—'

Svoboda sighed. 'Well, we can thresh out the details later. It won't be easy, whatever we decide. I can sympathize with Kivi's wish to spare his crew that sort of humiliation. He has their morale to worry about, the whole long way home.'

'And so you think, rather than chance a few of his men getting hurt, he will condemn us to almost sure failure?'

'Evidently.'

Judith shook her head. 'No. You're wrong, Jan. Consideration for his crew is one factor, yes. But Nils doesn't hate us. You've seen his rough side. I tell you, he was never anything but pleasant to me and the kids. He went out of his way to be pleasant. He won't leave us here to die. He isn't capable of it.'

Svoboda studied her a while. She wasn't beautiful, he thought; not in any conventional sense; but she was Judith, which was more. A wisp of an idea stirred. 'Are you certain?' he asked.

'Yes. As certain as I can be of anything, dear.'

'Okay. Then I begin to follow Kivi's logic. He doesn't believe we will stay here without that equipment. He expects we'll return with him to Earth. So of course he won't be a murderer. He can even tell himself he's doing what's best for us. Nobody denies that a lot of us would die, the first few years on Rustum, no matter what resources we had.'

'Yes, that must be his idea. You can't expect him to admit there's any sense in this colonizing.' Judith smiled faintly. 'Why, it'll be generations, no doubt, before we can build spaceships of our own.'

'There's more involved than that.' Svoboda looked at her till she squirmed uneasily. And the knowledge grew within him.

He had not imagined he could feel as much pity for a man as he did now, when he saw Kivi's real hope.

'Are we going to quit, then?' Judith whispered.

He answered absent-mindedly, his eyes never leaving her: 'I expect a majority will vote to do so.'

'And then the minority can hardly stay, can it?' Her lashes fluttered, as if seeking escape from his gaze. 'Everyone'll have to return.'

'How do you feel about that?'

'I ... oh ... of course I'm sorry, Jan. It seems so ... such a pity. And we sold everything to finance this, we'll come back poor, to an Earth full of strangers. And it meant so much to you.'

'But still, you wouldn't be altogether heartbroken. Would you?'

'What are you getting at?' she bridled. 'Quit staring at me!'

Svoboda clamped teeth together. There was no chance to explain. If any of the bored men outside the bunk curtain understood English, they were surely eavesdropping. To lay his plan out openly was to destroy its value.

Nor did he want to put it in words under any circumstances. Having seen the captain's weakness, he, Svoboda, should have done his best to forget what he saw – not use it so coldly against the man. He proceeded because he must, but the taste of his action was bad.

He took his wife's hands. 'Judith,' he said, 'I've something to ask. The hardest thing you ever did for me, and you've done more already than I had any right to expect.'

She grew steady again, though her smile was uncertain. 'What do you want?'

'However the vote goes – even if every single one of the others chooses to return – will you stay on Rustum with me and the kids?'

She drew a quick breath. He felt her fingers grow cold.

'I'm not out of my head,' he pleaded. 'We can do it. I swear we can. Or if not — Don't you remember what Earth was making Davy and Josy into?'

'Y-you always said —'

'Uh-huh. The old proverb. Better to die on your feet than

live on your knees.'

'A nice slogan,' she said bitterly. 'No. I won't.'

He made his final cast. 'Whatever happens,' he said, 'I am staying.'

Then he sat quiet. At last she pushed herself into the circle of his arms. 'All right,' she said.

He embraced her. To hell with any listening spacemen.

For a while they talked of what to do, if indeed they found themselves alone in High America. But Judith leaped from the subject with a strained little laugh. 'We may not have to,' she said. 'I may be able to talk Nils into salvaging the *Pioneer*.'

'Not if you approach him directly,' said Svoboda. 'He'll only tell you to be sensible, shut up and come home to Earth.'

'What is your salvage method anyhow, Jan?'

'Oh. That.' Svoboda smiled behind his bandages. 'An obvious one, actually. Somebody else would doubtless have thought of it if I hadn't. You know the mechanism that creates the Van Allen belts? Well, a planet's magnetic field is comparatively weak at any given spot, but covers an enormous volume of space. That's how it can trap those particles. A spaceship's protective magnetic screen can't possibly be that extensive, so it has to make up in sheer intensity. The forces which can deflect a fast-moving ion in a distance of a few kilometers are enormous. Only a thermonuclear power plant could generate them.

'Well, the *Ranger* is a metallic object, loaded with other metallic objects. A conductor. If you move any conductor across a magnetic field, or vice versa, you generate an EMF, whose value depends on the speed of the motion and the intensity of the field. Have you ever seen that classroom demonstration where a sheet of copper is dropped between the poles of a strong magnet? As it enters the field, its rate of fall slows down quite dramatically. The reason is that it cuts the lines of force. This sets up eddy currents in the copper. The energy of its fall is converted from velocity to electricity, and so eventually to heat.'

100

'Oh!' exclaimed Judith. 'Of course.'

'You see? We'll send the other ships of the fleet, turn by turn, past the *Ranger*, as fast and as close as possible. Which can be very fast and close indeed, under autopilot guidance, using a hyperbolic path opposed to the derelict's orbit. Thirty or forty K.P.S. should easily be attainable, I think. So ... their magnetic fields will slow the *Ranger*. It will lose energy, spiral into a lower orbit. After a sufficient number of passes, it'll be in a safe region and a repair crew can board it.'

'Why, that's a wonderful idea.' Judith hesitated. 'But how about the other ships? Will they be damaged?'

'Oh, they'll be decelerated, too. Newton's third law. But they'll make the actual passes in free fall, so it shouldn't impose any real strain. Besides, they won't be decelerated much. We'll fill their tanks, increase their mass ninefold. The *Ranger*'s tanks are all but empty.... Anyhow, we can't hurry the process. Eddy currents generate heat, which has to dissipate. We don't want to melt her.'

'You could get rid of the heat as fast as you want,' suggested Judith. 'Rig a pump on one spaceship and squirt water onto the derelict. It would boil off and take the heat with it.'

'Good girl. That angle occurred to me. There are other possibilities which may turn out to be preferable. The important thing is, we can recover the *Ranger*, if only Kivi —'

An accented voice beyond the curtains: 'Pleasse for Meester and Meesis Shofobota report to cappitain's office.'

Judith started. 'What?'

'I expected this,' said Svoboda. 'Someone listened to us and hurried to play informer. I'm as glad of it. Let's have this out at once.'

They went hand in hand down the passageways. His heart pounded thickly. A knock on the captain's door brought a harsh: 'Enter.' Svoboda let Judith go through, followed, and closed the door behind him.

The office, which was also the master's cabin, was small, crowded with booktapes and music spools, otherwise austere as any monkish cell. Kivi glared across the spider-legged magnetic board that was his desk. Somehow, subtly, he had become disheveled. His eyes were hot and dry.

'What's this nonsense about your staying?' he demanded.

'It's our business,' Svoboda answered.

'Yours, perhaps, You may leave your bones on Rustum if you wish. But your wife? Your children?' Kivi's face swung toward Judith. 'He cannot compel you. I offer my protection.'

She huddled close to her husband. 'Nobody is forcing me,' she whispered.

'But you are insane!' cried Kivi. 'This whole project was always a gamble against loaded dice. Now, without the *Ranger*'s cargo, the risks have shot up so far that most of your people will surely choose to return. Which makes death certain for any who stay behind.'

'Let me judge that for myself,' said Svoboda.

Kivi swiped the air, as if to strike him. 'Judith,' he said, 'you do not understand what is involved.'

Her head lifted. 'I understand what I promised at my wedding,' she told him.

Kivi sagged back. 'I am not being a monster,' he pleaded. 'I want to save my crew trouble, possible manslayings. That is why I would not hear any long-drawn recovery plans.'

That's one of your reasons, Svoboda thought.

'I will most gladly take your people home,' said Kivi. 'And, yes, I have money. I can help you, Judith, and your family get started afresh on Earth. What other use has a bachelor for his money?'

'No,' said Svoboda. 'The argument's closed. You have no legal power to make us leave. If you try to detain us, there will really be trouble between our parties!'

'Don't talk that way, Jan.' Tears stood in Judith's eyes. They broke off and floated toward the ventilator grille like tiny stars. 'Nils means well.'

Svoboda said with chosen cruelty: 'No doubt. So abide by your statistics, Kivi. Avoid whatever hazard there may

102

be to your crew. Let the colony break up. At worst, it should only cost four lives.'

And then, as Kivi's mouth grew unfirm and Svoboda saw victory, he would have given much not to have spoken.

The captain shivered. He looked at Judith, and away, and back again. 'You know I cannot do that,' he said. 'Very well, we shall salvage the *Ranger*. Now please leave me alone.'

Part 4: The Mills Of The Gods

1

'Nyaah, Nyaah, Nyaah!'

'Gawan, get inna back. Way inna back. You stink.'

'Yahh, he stinks. They grew him inna ole fertilizer tank, tha's what they did. A ole fertilizer tank.'

'Hey, Danny, who's your sister? That there cow your sister, huh, Danny?'

Jan Svoboda slapped the control panel with his open hand. 'Okay, enough,' he called. 'Quiet! Sit down.'

'Get 'at ole Danny way inna back,' said Pat O'Malley. 'I don't want any ole animal grown inna tank nex' to me.'

'Nyaah!' said Frank de Smet, and shoved. Danny Coffin went to his hands and knees in the aisle. Frank and Pat bounced from their seats and began to pummel him.

'That's *enough*!' Svoboda hit the panel again so it crashed under his palm. 'Next time this will be somebody's behind.' He half rose, turning around. A score of small boys fell silent and went back to their seats. Whenever his turn at being school-bus pilot came up, Svoboda soon got a reputation as a terror. That was in self-defense. The kids weren't really bad, but he ferried them between classes where they worked hard and homes where they worked harder. Somewhere along the line, they had to let off steam. Svoboda preferred not to have it let off while this old rattletrap was in the air.

'You're very mean to pick on poor Danny,' said Mary Lochaber, she of the starched blouse and the long golden curls. 'He can't help he was grown in a tank.'

'You pipe down too,' Svoboda said. 'You were grown in a tank yourself. It happened to be a uterus rather than an exogenetic apparatus. One of these days your parents will be adopting their own exogene baby, and he'll be exactly as

105

good as you are.' He hesitated. 'Not quite so lucky, is all. Okay, strap in.'

Danny Coffin snuffled and wiped his nose as he found a seat by Frank de Smet. He was a stocky dark-haired boy with a broad face and straight black hair: a touch of Oriental in his chromosomes. Since the school term began, he had grown very quiet. He hadn't fought back much when the others hit him, had mainly tried to ward the blows off.

I should speak to Saburo about him, Svoboda thought. Hirayama, who was his business partner, also taught judo in the upper grades. *A little special instruction might give that poor kid a chance to win respect.... Maybe not, though. With a fourth again as much gravity as Earth, Rustum's no place to use such tricks irresponsibly.* He shivered. Not long ago he had seen still another accident, a man fallen off a roof. Ribs had been driven into the lungs and the pelvis was smashed. On Earth, the victim would probably have broken nothing worse than a leg.

He touched the controls. Rotors grabbed air. The bus lumbered upward until the school, seen through windows, became a sprawl of sod roofs enclosing a dusty playfield. The few dozen timber buildings which were Anchor village dwindled with it, to a blot across the juncture of three bright threads. For here the Swift and Smoky Rivers running down from the Centaur Mountains in the west, joined to form the Emperor. Otherwise the landscape was green, with a faint overcast of metallic blue. Here and there stood a dark patch of woods, a pale patch where some farmer's corn and rye struggled to grow. Northward the country turned murky with forest; southward it rose in hills ever steeper and stonier until the Hercules range walled off that horizon.

This close to the autumnal equinox, Rustum divided its 62-hour rotation period almost evenly between day and night. The sun stood at late afternoon above the Centaurs, reddening their snowpeaks, casting their shoulders into black relief. Shadows stretched enormous across the land.

It was too big, that sun, and too bright, and at the same time too orange; it crept too slowly down a sky too wan a blue.

Or so those colonists felt who had been adults on Earth. The new generation, like Svoboda's busload of first-graders, found it merely natural. To them Earth was a word, a history lesson, a star which their elders named Sol. After seventeen years on Rustum – no, damn it, ten Earth-years – Svoboda found his own recollections of the mother planet getting blurred.

'Nyaah, teacher's pet. You hadda go squeal, didn'tcha? You wait till I get you tomorrow.'

'Belay that, Frank,' called Svoboda. The de Smet boy gulped and glared. The thick air of High America, more than twice the sea-level pressure of Earth, gave transmission so loud and clear that the children had never acquired those tricks of separating sound from noise which were second nature to their elders. This was not the first whisper Svoboda had overheard.

In his rearview mirror he saw Danny hug himself and sit back with his misery. The child's dark tight-fitting clothes marked him out to the eye as much as his status, the first exogene to enter school, did to the mind. The others were also dressed coarsely, by the standards Svoboda recalled on Earth, but some effort had been made to create a little gaiety of color and cut. Old Josh Coffin must think that was nearly as big a sin as happiness. Svoboda sometimes wondered whether the Coffins had not been the first to ask for their compulsory exogene because Teresa had failed to bear her own child, or because Joshua wanted still another duty to assume. Of course, after the adoption Teresa had proceeded to get pregnant anyway, a common occurrence. And this, instead of giving Danny some playmates at home, had presented him with a clutch of sibling rivals.

Poor kid. But it was nobody else's affair. As long as he wasn't obviously abused, his foster parents had a right to raise him as they saw fit, free from busybodies official and private. However – *I might consult Saburo. I just might.*

Svoboda turned his consciousness back to piloting. The route was changed each day – three five-hour classroom sessions, spaced around the clock – to divide the transit time as fairly as possible. He must guide himself by a complex pattern of landmarks, and be ready for air turbulence as well. At this pressure, even a light gust struck hard.

Not for the first time, the unoccupied part of him considered the interrelatedness of things. Old Torvald Anker, with his saying that 'Nothing is irrelevant,' would have been delighted by the examples Rustum presented. For instance, the connection between ecology and school buses. Because little native life on the plateau was edible, the colonists must raise Terrestrial crops. But because the ecology which supported those crops was not yet firmly established (consider, as one minor example, that local virus which attacked the nitrogen-fixing bacteria symbiotic with Earthly legumes), harvests were poor and it took many hectares to support a human. Therefore most of the colonists must be farmers, and live isolated in the middle of immense holdings. And thus they were dependent on aircraft – still so scarce and expensive as to be publicly owned – for their transportation beyond a horse's range. Especially the transportation of their children to and from classes. The effect of this, in turn, was to make school-bus piloting a duty for which those like Svoboda, who were not farmers, were drafted. Which tended to sharpen the conflict between professional classes.

Now and then Svoboda wondered if the freedom they said they had come here for might not already have soured.

Whatever route the bus took, Danny was always the last one off. The Coffins lived farthest out of anybody, near the edge of the Cleft. When Svoboda, today, set the bus down on their strip, Danny went past him without a word.

Teresa Coffin had stepped onto the porch as they landed. She had a baby in her arms. Another, lately begun to walk, hung onto her skirt. The level sunlight touched her hair with charitable bronze. She managed to wave. 'Hello,' she called. 'Want to stop in for a cup of tea?'

108

'No, thanks,' Svoboda answered, leaning out the window. 'Judith expects me home soon.'

Across the yard, bare trampled earth save where a plume oak spread its leafage, she smiled. 'Wedding preparations?'

He nodded. 'She's up to her ears in baking and sewing and Omniscience knows what else. I promised to help shift furniture before supper.'

'Well, tell her I'll bring those cookies I promised tonight, on the next Stein-Lake Royal bus. I wish I could do more, but—' Her gesture was wry. The Coffins had five youngsters now, including Danny, with a sixth on the way.

'Thanks. Everybody's being very helpful. I could wish it were in a better cause, though.'

'Why, Mr. Svoboda! Your own daughter's wedding!'

'Sure, sure. Of course I'm glad Jocelyn's hooked onto a decent lad like Colin Lochaber, and I want things to be done right, and so forth. But trying on this planet to imitate a Midlevel Earthly wedding reception – in harvest season at that—' Svoboda shrugged. 'It seems out of proportion.'

Teresa came down off the stairs, closer to him. Her face, lined and almost as weatherbeaten as his own, turned grave. 'That's where you're wrong,' she said. 'For us, these days, hardly anything is more important than a wedding.'

He thought of Jocelyn, David, Rustum-born Anton, the exogene infant Gail; his mind veered away from one small grave behind his orchard. At that, he and Judith were lucky. Most families had lost more. And they would continue to lose. There would be another Year of Sickness, another Peace Day blizzard, another who knew what. No doubt this was natural selection and would in time produce a race more healthy and gifted than Earth had known for centuries. But there were gray streaks in Judith's hair, and in his own. He had most of his strength yet, but hills had grown subtly steeper.

'Yes,' he said, 'you're doubtless right. And I don't deny it's nice to have a celebration occasionally. I didn't mean to sound like—' He stopped himself from saying 'your husband' and trusted she hadn't noticed. 'Anyhow,' he finished quickly, 'I've got to be on my way. So long.'

She smiled again. 'Till tonight. About 3900 o'clock.'

She must be looking forward to a visit with us, Svoboda thought. *An escape, for an hour or two.* He started feeling so sorry for her that he forgot about Danny.

2

Like most settlers' homes, this one was built of roughly dressed logs, bound together with steel and concrete against the great winds, with a storm cellar beneath. Long and low, cool despite the nearby sun, warm in winter, the house was not primitive. Besides electricity from the nuclear plant at Anchor, it had a solar collector which stored energy in an underground tank of superheated water. Light was fluorescent and heating radiant. But while power was plentiful, power tools were not. So much of the house must go to work space that the three boys bunked together in one room. Such conditions would be lavish for a Lowleveler on Earth, their father pointed out.

'But we aren't any old Lowlevelers,' Danny had said, in his first resentment when Ethan was moved in with him and Ahab.

'For which you can thank a just and merciful God,' Joshua Coffin had answered. 'You can even be thankful you weren't alive the first few years on Rustum, when we lived in tents and dugouts, and the rains came. I saw dying men, yes, women and children, lie in muddy water, with rain such as Earth never knew beating their faces.'

'Aw, that was so long ago,' Danny said.

His foster father's lips grew tight. 'If you think grown men have time to build an extra room whenever a new brat is born, you shall have to learn different,' he snapped. 'You can milk all the cows next choretime.'

'Joshua!' Mother cried. 'He's only a baby.'

'He's five Terrestrial years old,' Father answered. There was no more argument. Danny had learned better.

He liked the cows – they were warm and kind and smelled like summer – but there were a lot of them. Father spanked him when he didn't finish the job, before seeing that his fingers had gone too stiff to move. Then Father mumbled something like, 'All right, maybe it was too much,' and left the barn in a hurry. Afterward, unable to sleep for the pain in his hands, Danny had gotten up for a glass of water. From the dark hallway he saw Mother and Father in the living room. Father looked sad and Mother was stroking his hair. Since then Danny had never been sure if Mother really meant it when she stuck up for him.

And now he had to go to school. He'd rather have milked all the cows. He asked to, the first time he came home, after the other kids at recess had shouted, 'Stinky, Stinky, grown inna tank like a fat little piggy.' Not that he told his parents this. It was too monstrous. But he cried. Father told him to stop that nonsense and behave like a man.

Mother must have asked the teacher what was wrong. Mrs. Anthropopoulos knew the kids were riding Danny and told them to stop, but that only made them worse. ('You wait till I get you tomorrow,' Frank de Smet had whispered. There was a shed back of the playfield —) One day when Danny came home crying, Mother had packed a picnic lunch and they went off, the two of them, to the top of Boulder Hill. They sat on the big stones he often pretended had been rolled there by giants, and looked down on the house and barns, out across the blue-green pasture where the sheep seemed to be woolly bugs, the cornland where Father's tractor raised a plume of dust, and so on to the Cleft, which was the edge of the world. The wind ruffled a loose lock of Mother's hair and made the trees sigh around her voice. She talked low and carefully, as he had sometimes heard her talk when Father had gone off on one of his long walks by himself.

'Yes, Danny, you are different. It's not a bad difference. When you're older, you'll be proud of it. You, the first exogene on Rustum! There'll be others just like you, many others, and we're so glad to have you. Because we *need* you, Danny.'

But when he asked how come, she looked away. 'You're too young,' she said. Her fingers clenched together. 'When you've learned about heredity, then you'll know. That's one of the things you go to school for. To learn about, oh, everything. What we must know to live here on Rustum. And why we came. And what we must never forget, Earth and the people of Earth.... Danny, they pick on you because they don't understand either. They're scared, a teensy bit, of what they don't understand. You don't help them much, either. You should try to be more friendly. Not ask so many questions of the teacher. Join in their games, instead of going off by yourself and — Oh, I don't know. We came to Rustum to keep the right to be different. I suppose I shouldn't start the old cycle over again by telling you to conform simply because it's more comfortable.'

And this sounded so much like some of the things Father said, that Danny stopped liking the picnic and they soon went back to the house.

Later on, he learned more about the exogene tanks. There hadn't been room on the spaceships for livestock. So the seeds, the father seeds and mother seeds, were brought along instead. They were so tiny that you could carry enough seed to make millions of animals, cows, pigs, sheep, dogs, horses, poultry and everything. The seeds were kept alive, those long years in space, and later on in High America, by the same sort of deepsleep that kept the people alive. After everybody was settled on Rustum and ready for animals, the biotechs put the father seeds and mother seeds together and threw them in tanks till they had real baby animals.

Science class had lately gone down the street in Anchor to visit Biolab and see those tanks. The man in charge explained, though, that they weren't used this way any more, because the live animals had grown up and were now making little ones by themselves. He said many kinds had never been made at all, but the seeds were being kept in case those kinds were ever needed. He showed them pictures of some of those animals, snakes, elephants, mongooses, toads, ladybugs, and such.

So Danny understood exogenesis all right. He understood too that children grew in their mothers just like calves in

113

the cows, after their fathers had put in the father seed. Only ... not all children. Some were grown in tanks – the same tanks as the animals. Danny was the first. Why? When he asked, he was told that many different kinds of people were needed, but that didn't quite make sense. And why did every man and wife have to adopt at least one baby from a tank?

Once he overheard young Mr. Lasalle grumble to Father about that law, when they were on the same threshing crew. And Father had gotten mad and said, 'Have you no concept of civic duty?' So Father and Mother must have taken Danny because the law said they had to. They made his brothers and sisters themselves, so they must have wanted Ahab, Ethan, Elizabeth, Hope, and now this new one they had started, that would be born in a few more weeks. Danny was different. He was a civic duty.

Some people were nice to him. Mr. Svoboda, for instance. The kids didn't always hate Danny either. Most of the time they left him alone and he left them alone. But once in a while some of the boys beat up on him, like today. The bus had been a few minutes late, and there hadn't been anything else to do after class while they waited, so Frank started picking on Danny and Danny talked back and then a lot of them started teasing him.

He wiped his nose on his wrist, hoping Mother wouldn't see. She was talking to Mr. Svoboda and hadn't said hello to Danny. Maybe she didn't notice him. Maybe she didn't care. Danny slipped past her, into the house. He had to take his school clothes off and put on his farm clothes. It wasn't time for chores yet, but clothes were hard to make and hard to clean.

Ahab was on his bunk in the boys' room. He was not quite a year younger than Danny. (That was an Earth year, 139 days. They used the Rustum calendar mostly, but the old year lingered in such things as reckoning people's ages or when to have Christmas. Danny had often wondered about the powerful and mysterious Earth year, that marched around the seasons.) Ahab was brown-haired and slender, like all the *real* Coffin kids. 'Hi,' said Danny hopefully.

'Are you ever gonna get it when Father comes home,' said Ahab.

Danny's heart jumped. 'I haven't done nothing!'

'You haven't done nothing,' Ahab echoed. 'Sure. You didn't close the gate on the north six hundred. Mom says the gate was open.'

'I did! I did too! I always close the gate when I herd the sheep out there. Jus' before I left for school.'

'Mom says the gate was open. A catling could'a got in. Maybe a catling did get in. Maybe it's hiding in the woods and it's gonna kill the sheep till Father shoots it. You dumb ole sheep yourself!' Malice flickered on the round face. Ever since Ahab and Ethan had learned their big brother was an exogene (whatever that meant to them at their age), they had used it against him, because he was bigger and stronger and Mother was always more kind to him.

They didn't think how much more kind Father was to them.

'No!' Danny shouted. He ran from the room. Mother had come back inside and was changing little Hope.

'Mother, I didn't, I didn't. I know I closed the gate. I just know it.'

She glanced around. 'Do you?' she asked.

'I know!'

'Danny, dear,' she said gently, 'always remember how important objectivity is. That's a long word, but one reason why we came here is that people on Earth were forgetting it and this made them poor and miserable and unfree.' She left the baby on the couch, sat on her heels and took Danny by the shoulders and looked into his eyes. 'Objectivity means always trying to be truthful,' she said. 'Especially being truthful with yourself. That's the hardest and the most necessary.'

'I did close the gate. I always do. I know there's bad animals in the wild woods. I didn't forget.'

'Darling, the gate didn't leave itself open. You were there

115

last before me. I understand what happened. You don't like school, and you were thinking so hard about that that you forgot to close the gate. You didn't mean to leave it open, I know. But don't hide from the truth.'

He choked back the tears. Father said he was too old to be a crybaby like ... Ethan. 'M-m-maybe I did. I'm sorry.'

'That's a good boy.' She rumpled his hair. 'I'm not angry with you. I only wanted you to admit you'd made a mistake. We want people on Rustum never to get into the habit of lying to themselves. I'm very glad you didn't.'

'W-will Father know?'

She bit her lip. 'I don't see how to keep the others from blabbing,' she said, more to herself than him. Briskly: 'Never mind. I'll explain to him. It really wasn't your fault.'

'You always —' He couldn't finish, but pulled free of her and walked back to his room. She always said things hadn't been his fault, and Father never believed her.

'Boy, are you gonna get it,' said Ahab.

Danny ignored him. This was worse for Ahab than a blow. 'Nyaah, nyaah, nyaah, are you ever gonna get it, you old essogene,' he chanted. Danny changed clothes and walked back down the hall to the living room. Ahab didn't follow.

'Mother, can I go for a walk?'

Her eyes clouded. 'Again? I wish you didn't go walk so much alone. I thought —' She smiled very brightly. 'I thought perhaps after supper, when I take the bus to Svoboda's, I could let you off at the Gonzales'. You could play with Pedro.'

'Aww, no. Pedro just likes kid games. I can go by myself okay, Mother, honest. See, I'm wearing my bracelet.' Danny lifted his arm. The studded metal circlet gleamed on his wrist. Father had explained to him that this was a transistorized radio transmitter, and if he seemed to be lost or in trouble, any adult with a directional unit could go straight to where he was.

Those were pretty big words too. Danny was content to understand that if he wore the bracelet he could be found.

116

He'd gotten lost a couple of times already, in fact, and soon been found. Afterward Father had made hot cocoa for him and told him stories about King Arthur.

Today, mostly, he wanted to get away.

'Well ... all right,' said Mother. 'Remember, though, we have to feed and milk in about an hour. And afterward I'll be baking cookies for Miss Svoboda's wedding. Wouldn't you like to help?'

'Awww.' Danny didn't want to hurt her feelings, but that sort of thing was for girls. 'No, thanks, I guess. So long.'

He wandered out past the barn, over the rail fence of the clover meadow, among the scattered copses and tall grass of the undeveloped land – eastward, to his special favorite spot on the rim of the Cleft, which was the edge of the world.

3

As yet, High America had no formal government. Tele-visual discussion could settle what questions of policy arose. These were few, when most traditional functions of the state could be forgotten – military defense, for example – or else left to voluntary associations. Eventually there must be a more elaborate social structure; but this could evolve in an organic manner within the framework of Constitutionalist philosophy.

Or so the founders hoped.

However, somebody was needed to administer what laws there were, preside over debates, judge disputes, oversee such public services as medicine and education, and collect a tax to pay for them. This was the mayor, a full-time official elected every seven years (four and one-tenth Terrestrial years) if he didn't lose a vote of confidence in the interim. So far Theron Wolfe had kept that seat.

His office was on the second floor of the library, over-looking the Swift, which by day brawled green under a wooden bridge. Now at night, with neither moon up, he couldn't see the river. But his window stood open and he heard it. The plateau cooled off fast after dark, so it was as if the glacier-fed chill of the water blew in.

Joshua Coffin pulled his leather jacket more tightly about him. Wolfe, bulky and comfortable in a wool robe lined with slimspringer fur, cocked an eye toward the window. 'Close that if you wish,' he invited.

Coffin wrinkled his nose. 'Frankly, I'd rather be cold than breathe your smoke,' he said.

Wolfe looked at the stogie in his plump fingers. 'You must give us time,' he said. 'This is only the third season anyone has grown tobacco. I know it's strong enough to walk, but after so many years of abstention — Give us time to modify the soil, or the leaf, or something.'

'I should think the effort might better be put into improving our wheat.' Coffin compressed his lips. 'Never mind. I suppose you know why I have come.'

'Your kid is missing. I'm very sorry.'

'And no one will help look for him.'

'Oh, come. I was informed —'

'Yes, yes, yes. My neighbors beat the surrounding territory last night and today. But now they've quit.' Coffin struck one bony fist on his black-clad knee. 'They refuse to continue the search.'

Wolfe ran a hand through his hair, of which little remained, and adjusted the old-style spectacles on his nose. Anchor's lone optician was not yet prepared to make contact lenses. He puffed for a moment before he replied, 'If, as you say, bloodhounds failed to trace him past the rim of the Cleft, and no signal from his bracelet has been picked up —'

Coffin's voice grew as harsh as his features. He twisted his neck to look out the window, into darkness. 'I'll concede the dogs might lose his trail,' he said. 'It's so wet there, the odor probably would be washed off in a few hours. But the bracelet would not go out of order.'

'Even if – pardon me – he strayed into the woodlands and was set on by a catling? It might have swallowed the bracelet whole, and stomach acids —'

'Ridiculous!' Coffin's grizzled head swung back. The ceiling fluroros cast his eyes into shadow and gullied his face. 'The last big predator in that area was probably shot five years ago. If one had strayed in from the wilderness, the dogs would have known. They'd have raised a yell loud enough to wake Lazarus. And there's no plausible reason for the transmitter to stop functioning. The working parts are cased in steel which is cased in teflon. The unit is self-charging from solar energy. That's all the thing is: a device to convert incident radiation into a particular radio frequency. At night it runs on microcapacitors which have been sun-charged during the day. A portable locator unit can detect its emission at ten kilometers.'

'You needn't tell me,' said Wolfe mildly. 'I have grand-children.' He stroked his beard. 'What is your explanation, then?'

'That he went more than ten kilometers from home before he was missed, and never got back any closer to our extreme search point.' Coffin's finger stabbed at the mayor. 'And since we covered the plateau in a fifty-kilometer radius, that means he went down into the Cleft. My wife says he often sat beside it, daydreaming.'

'I know Danny,' said Wolfe, who knew everyone. 'He's got too high an IQ for his own good, but he's basically sensible. Would he go in that direction? I'm sure you've warned him.'

'Again and again.' Coffin looked away, braced himself, and looked back. 'My wife tells me he was in an unhappy mood when he left. The other children had been teasing him, and since he had forgotten to close a gate he ... he was afraid of my anger when I got back from harvesting. If he'd often indulged in fantasies about the land below the clouds —' He couldn't continue.

'Yes, that sounds plausible.' Wolfe squinted at the smoke which streamed from his lips before he added, 'As a matter of fact, I've already telespoken with several of your neigh-bors. They've explained their refusal to go very far down those cliffs. The risk is atrociously high. Especially now, in harvest time. If a rainstorm spoiled grain in the fields, the whole colony would have a hungry winter.'

'I'm prepared to risk *my* life and crops.' Coffin checked himself. Redness went up his gaunt cheeks. 'Forgive me,' he mumbled. 'My besetting sin. Spiritual pride. I appeal to you, Mayor, as ... as a father.'

'Spare the sentiment,' said Wolfe rather coldly.

'If you prefer. I'm prepared to do my duty by the boy, and I don't think I've yet gone to the limits of my duty. Is that an acceptable formulation?'

'Well ... what do you want me to do?'

'An aircraft —'

'I'm afraid that's impossible. You know what the turbu-

120

lence is like in the clouds – and with this air pressure behind it! None of those clumsy buses we use, stuck together in their old age with spit and baling wire, could survive. We do have some high-powered aircars, in pretty good shape; but we haven't the pilots. People like you and me have done so little flying since we came here, except for the most routine stuff, that we'd be sure to run afoul of the updrafts on the mountain slopes. Even our regular bus pilots would. I've consulted a few already. They tell me they could doubtless flit down to sea level if they didn't have to stay within ten kilometers of the slopes. Which, of course, an aerial searcher would have to. It's barely possible that O'Malley, Herskowitz, and van Zorn could survive a stunt like that. But they, as bad luck would have it, are off prospecting for copper in Iskandria. Half a planet away. Beyond reach of any radio apparatus or aircraft we've got here. Our transmitter can send a message that far, but their receivers wouldn't pick it up, except by some unlikely atmospheric freak.'

'I know!' Coffin interrupted the quick, smooth, political voice with a near shout. 'You think I haven't looked into the details? Certainly the searchers will have to go on foot. I'm ready to do so myself. But I realize it would be suicidal alone. Can you persuade someone to accompany me?' With evident distaste: 'You have considerable arts of persuasion.'

'It could be suicide for two, also,' said Wolfe, less surprised than Coffin had expected.

'Men have ventured several kilometers down into the Cleft before now, even below the clouds, and returned.'

'Proceeding carefully along the safest routes. You'd strike out in any direction you detected the signal.' Wolfe scowled. 'I'm sorry, Joshua, but the boy is probably dead. If he really went to a much lower altitude – and the gradient of the Cleft is so steep that ten kilometers of straight-line travel would drop him at least five kilometers – if he did that, then the air would get him.'

'No. Five kilometers below here, the pressure's enough to produce a degree of carbon dioxide intoxication in most people, I admit. But Daniel has a higher tolerance than average. He doesn't start yawning in a stuffy room, for instance. In any event, the poisoning isn't yet severe at that level, nor has nitrogen narcosis begun.'

'How about further on, though? Remember, air pressure rises almost exponentially as you approach sea level. Once he began to get weak and dizzy, he'd be nearly certain to stagger on downward till he dropped, rather than try to climb back up. Then there's the matter of food. By now he'd be so famished that death was a mercy.'

Coffin answered with equal grimness, 'The boy has been missing for a hundred hours, more or less. Allow another hundred for the searchers to overtake him. That may or may not be too short a time to starve to death, at his age. I'm sure he'd remember not to eat anything. I can pray God he's had sense enough, once he realized he was lost, to sit down and wait and conserve his strength. Can't I?'

Silence waxed in the room, except for the loud cold noise of the river. Then a circular saw in the lumberyard screamed. No one else was disturbed. The common pattern of life on Rustum had become an alternation of ten or eleven hours asleep with about twenty hours awake. Anchor was at work under the stars. But that shriek in the night made Coffin jerk where he sat, and roused Wolfe from his thoughts.

'I've been keeping track of this affair,' the mayor said. He had, indeed, carefully checked the records on Daniel Coffin, genetic, medical, school, and gossip. In an unobtrusive way, he kept track of everything. 'I expected you to come see me and suggest what you have. If I've spoken discouragingly, it was only because I wanted to make sure you really meant it.'

'If not, I wouldn't have come.'

Wolfe elevated his brows but answered merely: 'I've tried to get a man or two to stand by for such an expedition. Every farmer refused, pleading the harvest season as well as the hazard to his own life. They all see their first duty as being to their own families. Particularly when you, to be frank, have not made yourself the most popular man in High America. But now I'd like to approach someone in a non-agricultural profession. Jan Svoboda to start with.'

'The iron miner?' Coffin rubbed his long chin. 'I scarcely know him myself. My wife is friendly with his, though.'

'I bore that in mind when thinking about this, before you arrived. Chiefly, however, I considered the location of Svoboda's pit. It's on the northeast shoulder of the plateau, at three kilometers' lower altitude. He's used to higher air pressure, which will help some, and to the upper cloud environment, which will help still more.'

Wolfe shook his head. Light gleamed off the scalp. 'We know so very little about Rustum,' he mused. 'The first expedition barely scratched the surface of this one upland raised above this one continent. We colonists have been too busy establishing ourselves and surviving to explore beyond. I remember how glibly they used to talk on Earth about this planet or that planet, as if it were a kind of city – an entire world! Svoboda's special knowledge, his years of experience, may fill one paragraph in the hundred-volume geographical text which may someday describe Rustum.'

'Stop fiddling around with the obvious!' Coffin grated.

'Okay.' Wolfe's big-bellied form rose behind the desk and moved with surprising lightness toward the door. 'My official aircar's parked outside. Let's go see Svoboda.'

4

Raksh, the outer moon, was rising as Wolfe landed. Being at closest approach and nearly full, it showed twice the angular diameter of Luna seen from Earth, a mottled coppery shield whose light limned the distant snowpeaks and glittered off hoarfrost on grass. And it came from the west. Slowly, slowly; it needed 53 hours to complete an apparent period, almost twice as long as its orbital time around Rustum – so that you saw it change size and phase while hanging in the sky. Tiny Sohrab would come from the west too but cross low in the south, and fast enough for a man to watch.

With such a double spectacle up there, one might have expected the stars to write Alpha and Omega. But they were only somewhat dimmed by the thicker air. Except for the Eridanus region, not visible from High America anyway, the constellations were Orion, Draco, the Great Bear, Cassiopeia, all the remembered images of night on Earth. An astronomer would have been needed to spot the slight distortions. (Well, Sol itself did lie just above Boötes, when Raksh didn't swamp its feeble glimmer.) Twenty light-years, four decades of travel, amounted to little in the galaxy.

Coffin shivered as he stepped from the car. His breath was white under the moon. The luminance poured cold and unreal across the garden surrounding the house, edged the long leaves of a plume oak with silver, and cast the shadow of a gimtree copse over a thinly frozen pond. Abandoned in autumn but with some of its luminous fungi still alive, the nest of a bower phoenix hung in that grove like a goblin lantern. A glow wing flitted blue across the forest background, from which came the trill of a singing lizard, eerily like three bars of some old Scotch melody. The wind, slow and heavy, rustled withering leaves with a sound which was not like October in New England, nor like anything Earth had ever heard.

Nonetheless – in contrast to spring and summer, when the wildlife of Rustum filled each night with trilling and calling and croaking – it was quiet. Boots rang loud on the frosty soil. Coffin was more grateful than he cared to admit when the door of the house opened and warmth and yellow light spilled over him.

'Why ... come in,' said Judith Svoboda. 'I wasn't expecting—'

'Is Jan home?' asked Wolfe.

'No, he's at the mine.' She watched them for a moment which grew. The color began to leave her face. 'I'll call him,' she said.

While she was at the visiphone, Coffin sat down on the edge of a chair. Wolfe, more at ease, made a couch groan beneath his weight. This living room was larger than average, so much like memory with its rough ceiling beams and stone fireplace and rag rugs that Coffin must bite his lip and remind himself that such homes had vanished from Earth. Now that a photoprinter was available to make full-size copies of micro material, private libraries were coming back. The Svobodas had well-filled shelves, though this was offset by authors like Omar Khayyam, Rabelais, and Cabell, right out where children could read them.

Judith looked in. 'He'll be back as soon as he can,' she said. 'He has to shut down the automatic scoop himself, because Saburo's busy on the digger pilot. Something wrong with its computer.' She hesitated. 'Can I make you some tea?'

'No, thank you,' said Coffin.

'Yes, by all means,' said Wolfe. 'And if any of your famous berry biscuits happen to be lying neglected—'

She threw him a smile more grateful than gracious. 'Surely,' she said, and vanished into the kitchen. Wolfe stretched out an arm to the nearest bookshelf, chose a volume, and lit a fresh cigar. 'I don't imagine I'll ever understand Dylan Thomas,' he said, 'but I like the words

125

and anyhow I doubt if he intended to be understood.'

Coffin sat straight and looked at the wall.

Presently Judith came back with a tray. Wolfe sipped aloud. 'Excellent,' he declared. 'You, my dear, have the honor of being the first lady on Rustum to re-invent the true art of making tea. Quite aside from the fact that the leaves acquire peculiar flavors when grown here, one must allow for a twenty-degree difference in the boiling of water. What blend do you use? Or is it a secret?'

'No,' she said absently. 'I'll copy the recipe for you. . . . Excuse the mess. Wedding preparations, you know. Party tomorrow after sunrise. But of course you both have your invitations —' She broke off. 'I'm sorry, Mr. Coffin.'

'No offense,' he said, realized that was the wrong thing, and couldn't find any way to make it up.

She didn't seem to notice. 'I've been in touch with Teresa,' she said. 'I don't think I could take such news as bravely as she has.'

'If this had to happen,' said Coffin, 'thank God it was not to a natural child.'

Judith flushed indignantly. 'Do you think that makes any difference – to her?' she exclaimed.

'No. Pardon me.' He rubbed his eyes with thumb and forefinger. 'I'm so tired I hardly know what I'm saying. Don't get me wrong. I intend to keep searching till . . . at least till we find out what happened.'

Judith glanced at Wolfe. 'If Danny is dead,' she said in a voice not quite level, 'I think you should arrange for Teresa to get another exogene as soon as possible.'

'If she wants one,' said the mayor. 'He lived past the minimum required age. She doesn't have to take another.'

'She does, down inside. I know her. If she doesn't ask, force her to. She's got to see that she didn't . . . didn't fail.'

'Think so, Josh?' inquired Wolfe.

Coffin's ears felt hot. They were discussing his private business. But they meant well, and he dare not offend Jan Svoboda's wife. 'In any event,' he managed to say, 'I believe such an adoption would be our duty.'

'Duty be damned!' she flared.

In his weariness, the old habit of a celibate spaceman took over, treating women like retarded children, and he said, 'Don't you understand? Three thousand colonists don't furnish a large enough gene pool to insure species survival. Particularly on a new planet, where a maximum variety of human types is needed so the race can adapt itself in the minimum number of generations. The exogenes, as they are begotten and adopted and reach maturity, will eventually total a million additional ancestors for the ultimate human stock. They are necessary.'

'Judith does have an education,' said Wolfe.

'Oh. Of course. I didn't – I mean —' Coffin clenched his fists. 'I beg your pardon, Mrs. Svoboda.'

'Quite all right,' she said, though without warmth. He didn't think she was miffed at his *faux pas*. But what, then? That he had called the exogenetic babies a duty? Well, weren't they?

Silence stretched. It was a relief to hear Jan Svoboda arrive. The sound was a descending whine, which became a steady murmur as the rail car balanced on its gyros. With transportation aforethought, he had built his house next to the ore-carrying line between his iron pit and the steel mill in Anchor.

The whine resumed and dwindled as he sent the car back. He stalked in. His pants were smeared with oil, his tunic red with hematite. 'How do you do,' he said roughly.

Coffin rose. Their handshake was brief. 'Mr. Svoboda —'

'I heard about your boy. It's very sad. I'd have come and helped look for him myself, but Izzy Stein told me your neighbors could cover the possible territory.'

'Yes. If they had been willing to do so.' Coffin blurted out what he had said to Wolfe.

Svoboda's glance went to his wife, and the mayor, and back to his wife. She stood with one hand to her mouth, watching him from enormous eyes. His own countenance went blank and he said without tone: 'So you want me to come along with you, down into the Cleft? But if the boy

127

went that way, he's dead by now. I hate to put it so cruelly, but he is.'

'Are you certain?' asked Coffin. 'Can you stay home and be convinced you might not have saved him?'

'But —' Svoboda jammed hands in pockets, stared at the floor and back again. A muscle jumped at the angle of his jaw. 'Let's keep on being brutally honest,' he said. 'In my opinion, the probability that the boy can be found alive is vanishingly slight, while the probability that one or more of the searchers will be injured, or killed, is quite large. It seems poor economy on Rustum, where every hand is needed.'

Anger sprang within Coffin: 'Yes, Mr. Svoboda, I would call that kind of honesty brutal.'

'Like your argument during the Year of Sickness that we shouldn't put cairns on the dead, but let the carrion devils dig them up and eat them?'

'We were far more shorthanded then. And it didn't matter to the dead.'

'It did to their families. Why pick on me, anyhow, for Christ's sake? I'm busy.'

'Preparing for a wedding!' Coffin snorted.

'It can be postponed ... if you must go,' Judith whispered.

Svoboda went over to her, took both her hands in his and asked most softly, 'Do you think I should?'

'I don't know. You have to decide, Jan.' She pulled free of him. 'I'm not brave enough to decide.' Suddenly she went out of the room. They heard her run down the hall toward the bed chamber.

Svoboda started to follow, halted, and turned on the others. 'I stand by my judgment,' he snapped. 'Has anyone got the nerve to call me a coward?'

'I think you should reconsider, Jan,' said Wolfe.

'You?' Svoboda was astonished.

Coffin almost echoed him. Both men stared at the portly form on the couch. This was the mayor who had voted against burial cairns in the evil year; who had talked the

128

farmers out of a hornbeetle extermination program on the ground that it was more expedient they suffer known crop damage than future generations suffer the unknown consequences of a possibly upset ecology; who had bribed Gonzales to drop an impractical scheme to dam the Smoky River by finding for Gonzales in a lawsuit; who had kept young Tregennis from starting a washing-machine factory he felt would at this stage use too many of the colony's resources, by acquiring Tregennis' capital in an astronomical poker game — 'I don't believe your chances would be that bad,' said Wolfe.

Svoboda rumpled his hair. Sweat began to glisten beneath it. 'I'm not abandoning the kid,' he protested. 'If I thought his chances – of being alive – were any good, of course I'd go. But they aren't. And I've got a wife, and two of my own children are still small, and — No. I'm sorry as hell. I won't sleep decently for a long time to come. But I am not going down into the Cleft. I haven't the right.'

Coffin dragged the admission from himself: 'If that's the way you want it, I'll have to believe you're acting in good conscience.' Weariness settled on his shoulders like a block of iron. 'Let's go, Mr. Wolfe.'

The mayor rose. 'I'd like a word with Jan in private, if neither of you mind,' he said. He took his host's arm, led him into the hall and closed the door behind them.

Coffin flopped into a chair. His knees had been about to give way. O God, to be in space again! His head rolled loosely against the chair back and he closed his eyes, which were burning in their sockets.

His hearing was better than average. When the lowered voice of Wolfe still reached him through the door, he tried to stand up and go out of earshot, but will and strength had left. It didn't matter. Nothing mattered. He heard the mayor say:

'Jan, you've got to do this. I'm sorry to postpone your daughter's marriage and sorrier yet to hazard your life, but you're damn near the only man who might rescue that boy – or find his body – and get back alive. It has to be you.'

'It won't be.' Svoboda spoke sullenly. 'You can't compel me. The group has no constitutional claim on the individual except in case of clear and present public danger. Which this is not.'

'Your reputation, though —'

'Nonsense. You must know yourself, every man in High America will understand me.' Svoboda's control began to crack. 'Jesus, Theron! Lay off! We've come such a long way together ... since we first started organizing people on Earth. ... You wouldn't ruin it now, would you?'

'Of course not. I meant the reputation I want you to get: a hero. Which, apart from egotism and the pleasure given your family, can be very useful. With our labor shortage, a boss who wants workers must be a popular figure. You've told me you want to expand your operations.'

'I don't want to that much. Theron, the answer is no, and it hurts too much for me to keep repeating it. Go home.'

Wolfe sighed. 'You force my hand. I don't always enjoy blackmailing people.'

'Huh?'

'I know about you and Helga Dahlquist, one night last summer.'

'Wha-wha-what – You're lying!'

'Whoa, son. Information that reaches me stays there ... most of the time. But I've got ways to prove what I claim. Now naturally I'd hate to hurt your wife —'

'You lousy fat slug! It didn't mean anything. We were both drunk and – and – her husband too. You'd hurt him still worse than Judy. You know that? He's a good fellow. I've been sorrier on his account, even, than on my wife's. It was just one of those damned impulses – Helga and I — You'll keep your flapping mouth shut!'

'Certainly. If you agree to try and rescue Danny.'

Coffin attempted once more to rise. This time he succeeded. He should not have heard that conversation. He went over to the window and stared out, hating Rustum, despising Svoboda, tasting the full measure of his own blood guiltiness.

The door opened at his back. Svoboda came through. He was saying, with a touch of merriment that completely baffled Coffin: '– and thanks. You're a rat, but I'm not too sorry you are.' He paused. 'I'll be at your house an hour before sunrise, Mr. Coffin.'

5

The east side of the tableland called High America did not slope off like the other edges, but fell with an unscalable abruptness. Kilometer after kilometer the palisades marched, a sheer hundred meters down to talus slopes which in turn were cut off by a rank of precipices, and so on till clouds hid the lower steeps. Only where a fault had split the mountains and a hundred million years had eroded the resulting gash could men find a way. Few had tried it, and none had gone far.

Where it notched the plateau rim, the Cleft was five kilometers wide. As it slanted down, it broadened. Though he had often seen the view, Svoboda parted a screen of cinnabar bush and looked with awe.

Overhead arched the dawn sky, purple in the west where a last few stars blinked above the hump of the Centaurs, clear blue at the zenith which a now waning Raksh had approached, almost white in the east. The upland behind him lay huge, shadowy, and still; treetops were hoar where they caught the light. The cliff toppled at his feet, gray-blue streaked with mineral reds and yellows, spotted with bushes that had somehow rooted themselves fast, down and down to the sharded rock of a slope which itself tumbled downward. Directly across from him lay nothing but cold air, until the eye found a crag upreared on the opposite verge and saw the first sunbeams throw shadows of infinite complexity over its face. A spear-fowl, big as an Earthly condor, hovered out there. Its feathers were like shining steel.

'This way,' said Coffin. His voice was too loud, ugly in that silence. Pebbles kicked from his boots went rattling and bouncing to the cliff brink, and over.

Svoboda trudged behind. The pack on his shoulders and the gun at his hip seemed to weigh him down already. Like the other man, he was clad for a rough hike, in homesewn shirt and pants of drab green; but his messkit and sleeping gear would have made Daniel Boone envious. The first expedition and the subsequent colonists had developed certain wilderness techniques.

The trouble was, they were only appropriate to the plateau. Men had taken quick peeks at the forest beneath the clouds, shuddered, and returned. There was more than enough to do on the heights, without pushing into lands where you could scarcely breathe. Last year John O'Malley had taken an aircraft down to sea level and come back with nothing worse than a severe headache; but few people had that much tolerance to such pressures of carbon dioxide and nitrogen. O'Malley himself doubted he could have survived many days.

And so Danny – Svoboda grimaced. He didn't want to see the boy's corpse. It would be rotten, probably, if the carrion devils or the corvines hadn't found it.

'Here,' said Coffin. 'The dogs traced him this far.'

Svoboda looked closely. They had reached the middle of the notch. Boulder-strewn, it wound steeply downward, its slant sides rising to form cliffs. At the bottom of vision were the clouds.

He had ignored them when he first gazed over the Cleft. They were nothing but a whiteness far under his feet. But now they lay ahead. The first semicircle of e Eridani was visible, blinding in the east above a billowing snowlike plain. Blue shadows crawled toward him, kilometers in length. Mist began to pour up the canyon, filling it from side to side, a gray wall whose top faded to gold smoke. Svoboda caught his breath. He hadn't watched sunrise over the Cleft for years. It brought back to him how much else was beautiful here, the summer forests, Elvenveil Falls, Lake Royal turquoise in the morning and amethyst in the evening, a double moonglade shivering on the Emperor River ... in spite of everything, he was glad he had come to Rustum.

He did not want to end his days in the Cleft.

'Daniel used to sit on that rock overgrown with lyco-poid,' Coffin pointed. 'I think he must have developed some wild ideas of what lay back of the clouds. At least, he used to spin such fantasies when he was little. Naturally, I dis-couraged that.'

'Why?' asked Svoboda.

'What?' Coffin blinked. 'Why discour — But that sort of thing, it isn't truthful! You, as a Constitutionalist —'

'Anker never said fun and fantasy were untruthful,' Svoboda snapped. He reined in his temper. 'Well, let's not argue theories of child rearing. Have you been this way before?'

Coffin's long gaunt head nodded. 'I've explored a couple of kilometers down in detail, and went about twice that far yesterday, searching. Beyond —' He shrugged. 'We'll have to see.' He took a location bracelet from his pocket and laid it on the rock from which Danny had watched the golden smoke. A series of such radio markers would enable them to find their way back, and to orient themselves. 'Let's go.'

He started along the bottom of the gorge. Svoboda fol-lowed. The fog poured like a river to meet them, hiding the sun again. Drawn upward by the warming of the air, the vapors would hang around the plateau brim for hours. The men couldn't wait that long. In any event, they would probably have to penetrate such mists. Hotter than Earth and with a larger ocean surface, Rustum had a semi-per-manent cloud layer in its atmosphere. The uplands which poked beyond this were a special climatic zone, normally arid. High America was fortunate in getting the runoff from the still taller peaks of Centaur and Hercules, and thus a decent amount of moisture. What scanty information was available suggested that the cloud stratum also separated two distinct life zones.

Svoboda concentrated on keeping his feet. Stones twisted beneath his soles and materialized in front of his toes with fiendish precision. Huge drifts of boulders must be scrambled across; crags must be gone around; spike-hedge must be pushed through; bluffs must be slid down. The air closed in until he walked through dripping, swirling gray, where Coffin was a shadow ahead of him and pinnacles were briefly seen to right and left like hooded ghosts.

After a long while he called: 'Any trace on the locator?'

Automatically Coffin glanced at the black box strapped on his pack. Tuned to the wavelength of Danny's bracelet, the directional antenna wobbled randomly about on its swivel. 'Certainly not,' he answered. 'We haven't even come as far as I did yesterday. I'll tell you if I get a signal, never fear.'

'You needn't take that tone,' bridled Svoboda. 'You asked me for help.'

'Danny asked both of us for help.'

'This is no time for sentimentalism. Especially as sticky as that.'

Coffin halted and turned around. For a moment his face was thrust livid out of the fog, and one fist doubled. Svoboda's heart lost a beat. *I'd better aplogize —*

'Strengthen me, God,' said Coffin. He resumed walking. *Not to that prig,* Svoboda decided.

As they went on, quick violent winds boomed in their ears and dashed the fog against them, without being able to blow it away. The ground grew wetter until it gleamed in the thick twilight. Trickles ran down every stone, rivulets coursed between, springs welled forth within meters of each other. The loud ringing noise of waterfalls could be heard from cliff walls invisible in the roiled vapors. But there were no more plants. The men seemed to be the only life remaining.

'Stop a minute,' said Svoboda at last.

'What's the matter?' Coffin's voice sounded muffled by the dankness.

'We're into the permanent clouds. You ever been this far?'

'No. What of it?'

'Well, my own digging is at a slightly higher altitude than this, thank fortune. But occasionally, for one reason or another, I have to come down to this level or a bit lower.

135

And then there are the reports of the previous exploratory descents. We're entering the dangerous area.'

'What's there to be afraid of? This region is dead.'

'Not quite. In any event, the footing will be slippery, the wind gusts terrific, the gradient steeper yet, and ourselves half blind. We'd better plan our next moves in advance. Also, it's time for a rest and a snack.'

'While Danny may be dying?'

'Use your brains. We can't help him if we wear ourselves out.' Svoboda hunkered down and removed his pack. After a moment Coffin joined him, grudgingly. They spread a pliosheet to sit on, broke out a chocolate bar, and ignited a therm capsule under the tea-kettle.

There was no medical reason to boil water here – or, probably, in the most fetid lowland swamp. The few native diseases to which humans were subject all seemed to be airborne. It was the good side of the biochemical coin, the bad side being that little native vegetation had been found which was edible by man. A number of animals were, since the stomach can break down most exotic proteins, but none met the complete requirements of nutrition and many were as poisonous as the average plant. The bad of the meat coin was, obviously, that some Rustumite carnivores had discovered they liked human flesh.

Svoboda wanted tea because he was cold and wet and tired.

'There's considerable water erosion in the cloud belt,' he said. 'Crumbly rock. We'd better clamp on our spike soles and rope ourselves together.' He sighed. 'No offense, but I wish I had a more experienced partner than you.'

'You could have co-opted Hirayama, could you not?'

'I didn't. He'd have come if I'd asked, but I didn't ask. Haven't even told him.'

Coffin clamped his jaws. There was stillness except for the rush and whistle of wind, the dripping and chuckling of water. When he had himself under control, he said in a flat voice, 'Why? The more in this party, and the more skilled they are at mountain climbing, the better our chances.'

136

'Yeh. But Saburo is a family man too. And if I should die, he'd keep the mine going, and thus provide my own family with an income.'

'Your survivors could work. Jobs go begging on this planet.'

'I don't intend that Judy should have to get a job. Nor my kids till they're grown.'

'In other words, you'd rather have them be parasites?'

'By God —!' Svoboda half rose. 'You take that back or I start home this minute.'

'You can't,' Coffin snarled.

'The hell I can't.'

'You and Mayor Wolfe — Be glad your sin isn't punished worse than this.'

'Why, you bluenosed, keyhole-peeping— Put up your fists! Go on, get up and fight before I kick you in the belly!'

Coffin shook his head. 'No. This is no place for a fight.'

The mist swirled and eddied. The tea-kettle began to boil. Coffin charged the pot. Svoboda stood over him, breathing hard.

Slowly, Coffin's head drooped. Shame stained his cheeks. 'I apologize,' he muttered. 'I didn't intend to eavesdrop. I couldn't help overhearing. None of my business. I certainly ought not to have mentioned it. I won't, ever again.'

Svoboda struck a cigaret, squatted, and did not speak until the tea was ready and a full cup in his hand. Then, his eyes avoiding the other man, he said: 'Okay, agreed, this is no place to quarrel. But don't call my family parasites. Is it parasitic for a woman – a widow – to keep house and raise the kids? Is a school child or a student a parasite?'

'I suppose not,' said Coffin without great sincerity.

'Quasi-cultural conflict between us,' Svoboda remarked, trying to smile and ease the atmosphere. 'You farmers tend to be at loggerheads with us entrepreneurs because we compete with you for machinery, which is still at a premium. But there's a basic difference of attitude developing, too. Inevitably so, I guess. By and large, the most scientifically

137

oriented people have tended to go into non-agricultural lines of work. And they're a touch more pragmatic and hedonistic, I suppose. I've often heard farmers and ranchers worry about High America evolving into another mechanical, proletarianized Earth.'

'That's one reason I chose to farm, in spite of my earlier background,' Coffin admitted.

Svoboda stared into the blowing blindness. 'We needn't worry about that for centuries yet,' he said. 'Not with a whole world to spread into.'

'But we haven't got a world,' Coffin pointed out. 'We have a few uplands, most of them deserts. We'll fill them with people in another several generations. Then what? We have to provide against that day. Build a culture that won't fall into the same trap as Earth.'

'Yes, I've heard that line of reasoning before. Myself, I don't see how you can force the evolution of a culture along present lines without losing the freedom we came here to preserve.'

'Maybe so. If you ask me, you overrate freedom dangerously – but then, I never was a Constitutionalist. I can tell you for certain that freedom requires elbow room. How can a man even be an individual, if there's no place he can go to be alone with his God? and High America will run out of elbow room in a century or two.'

'Someday there'll be people who can live at sea level. Nature will select for such a breed.'

'A thousand years hence? That's not much use. Your libertarianism, my individualism (they are not identical), they will be long extinct.' Coffin's own eyes followed Svoboda's, into the wet nothingness ahead. 'I wonder what men will find, though. Down there.'

'It's anybody's guess.'

'Er – I thought I heard you remark, a while ago, this cloud stratum has life forms of its own.' Coffin seemed eager to talk impersonally.

Svoboda was glad to oblige. 'Haven't you heard of the nebulo-plankton? Well, I don't suppose you would have,

138

since it rarely comes this high. Not much is known about it anyway, except that it consists of tiny organisms, plant, animal, and intermediate, that float within the permanent cloud band. My personal theory about them is that wind scours fine particles off surface rocks and the dense air carries them up to this level, where the water drops dissolve out some of their minerals. I don't suppose it could happen on Earth, but here where you have a thick permanent stratum and an atmosphere that can uphold larger drops of water, you do get an appreciable concentration of mineral ions in the clouds. And of course there's the CO_2 and, though you'd hardly think so, abundant sunlight. So my guess is that microscopic life forms developed to use this thin mineral soup; and slightly larger species developed to feed off them; et cetera. It's a very tenuous blanket of life, as you'd expect. I'll be surprised if it averages ten pinhead-sized bits of living mineral thistledown per cubic meter. But there is life. There's even a giant form, bigger than a man in volume if not weight, which grazes on it.'

'Do you mean the air porpoises? I've heard vaguely of them.'

'They aren't seen often. I've glimpsed them a few times over the years. In fact, there was one hanging around near the mine only yesterday. But it stands to reason, if they live off the nebulo-plankton they must be a rare species. I've watched them through binoculars. They're shaped like fat cigars and seem to propel themselves by a sort of jet. My guess, again, is that they keep aloft by filling a big external bladder with biologically generated hydrogen; and that they suck in air, retain the plankton, and blow the air out behind for propulsion. Slow, stupid, and harmless. But damned interesting. I'd love to dissect one.'

Coffin nodded. 'However low the average density of plankton,' he pointed out, 'turbulence is bound to produce local concentrations. Also, where an updraft habitually moves along a bare mountainside like this, the clouds will be more mineralized and can support more organisms. That may be what attracts the porpoises.' He hesitated. 'Is

139

there any harm in breathing the plankton, do you think?'

'I wouldn't make a habit of it,' Svoboda said. 'Silicosis might become a distinct hazard. But merely passing through now and then should be quite safe. The previous explorers weren't bothered. Oh, conceivably some of the species contain some chemical which'll cause the men to develop lung cancer in another decade. Who knows? But I doubt that.'

Coffin shrugged. 'In a decade the hospital should have a full battery of cancer cures.' He drained his cup. 'Shall we go?'

Svoboda made him wait, fuming, for half an hour of rest. Then they donned their spikes, repacked their stuff, and roped themselves together. Svoboda took the lead, groping over declivities unknown to them both, which plunged ever more sharply between the invisible cliffs. The fog pressed close; the rivulets joined to make a stream beside which the men must pick their way. That water ran gray-green with mineral dust, white-streaked and noisy with haste, and cold.

Time was soon lost for Svoboda. Nothing remained but the weariness in shoulders and knees, the clamminess of garments, the buffet of winds, slipperiness underfoot and dankness in his nostrils. But he kept a memory of the report made by the exploratory climbers. They had had no means of drawing an accurate map, but they had noted what landmarks they could. Where the stream went over a high precipice, one must veer aside and follow a ledge ... and didn't he now hear those cataracts, bawling and booming in the clouds?

Yes. He signalled a stop when he came to the place. Ahead of him the drenched, rock-littered ground came to an end, nothing but mist to be seen, as if he stood on the rim of Ginnungagap. On his left the river dashed itself over that brink and was lost to view; only the noise that drifted back up, rumbling and echoing through the wind, gave proof that it had not been sucked away by the fog. On his right, vague and huge, a promontory thrust beyond the cliff

140

like a guard tower adjoining the outer wall of some titan's castle. That rock was pocked and scarred with weathering. A fault, slanting downward out of sight, made a sort of trail. Under that narrow ledge, the promontory dropped sheer into invisibility. But the explorers had made an echo estimate of its height. A hundred and fifty meters, was that it?

Svoboda indicated the outthrust. 'There's the only way to proceed further,' he said. 'Nothing yet on your radio locator, I suppose? Then the kid must have taken yonder trail. He can't be behind us in the Cleft, off to one side, because we've passed within a ten-kilometer radious of all that territory. Unless his bracelet isn't working.'

'You needn't waste time repeating the obvious,' Coffin grunted.

After a glance at the hollowed face beside him, Svoboda decided not to resent that. He said gently: 'So far the trek hasn't been too difficult for an active boy unencumbered by a pack. I can well imagine him coming this far, attempting to run away to fairyland. Because he could always find his way back if he wanted to. But when he arrived here —'

'He might wilfully continue.'

'I doubt it. Look, he'd have come far enough so the exercise would have eased his mood. In fact, he'd be cold and hungry. Now that's a slow, difficult, obviously dangerous trail there. And most especially – night must have been coming on by then. Danny wasn't old enough, I guess, to foresee being caught here by sundown; but he was certainly able to see that once he started along the ledge, he'd not get back soon or easily.'

'So why did he continue? Well, I must admit I'm puzzled, when you put it in such terms. He ... he isn't a bad boy, you know. He cares for Teresa, at least, if not for — No, I don't understand either.'

Svoboda gathered courage to declare what Coffin was unable to: 'If he ventured a short ways out on the ledge, slipped and fell — It's a long way down. His bracelet could have been smashed on a rock when he landed.'

Coffin didn't reply.

'In which case we'll never find him,' said Svoboda.

'He could have negotiated the trail,' said Coffin, as if choked.

'In the dark? And now be more than ten straight-line kilometers beyond *this* point? I'll give you even odds that that means thirty kilometers on the ground. No, I'm sorry, but let's use our brains. Danny's at the bottom of this cliff.'

Svoboda paused. 'He must have died instantly,' he added in a low voice.

'We don't know for certain,' Coffin said. 'We have supplies to continue till night and start back at sunrise. We can't do less.'

Why the hell should I risk my neck? Svoboda thought. *To soothe your own bad conscience for the way you treated him? There's no other reason to carry on this farce.*

Except Theron and his filthy blackmail. Svoboda gasped with anger. 'Okay,' he said. His instructions in technique were curt and scornful.

They started off across the rock face. The falls were soon hidden, their sound muffled in the curdling grayness; but condensed moisture streamed over the promontory and dripped off the ledge. Sometimes the trail was broad enough for walking, sometimes it narrowed so that a man must press his face to the stone and shuffle sideways. There'd be no chance to eat until they reached the slope below, and Svoboda remembered from the report of the explorers that that would take hours. He should have called lunchtime before they started on this path. But in his rage he had forgotten. Now his stomach growled for him. He began to feel a little weak, and must battle against the fear of losing hold in a moment of dizziness or a sudden flow of wind.

Losing hold and falling. Ten or fifteen seconds to know he was a dead man, and then spattered into oblivion.

Like Danny, who had tasted horror as the air shrieked past —

Svoboda whirled.

The scream came again. The birds which swooped upon

142

him, crying from throats like brass, were the color and hook-beaked shape of spearfowl. But their wings had twice the span. They rushed at the men so swiftly that there was no time to draw weapon.

Talons smote Svoboda on the breast. A beak tore at his pack. He reeled from the blow and went over the edge.

Coffin stamped hard. His spikes drove into cracks in the stone. Their blades expanded from the slots and held him fast. Svoboda's weight slammed against him. He threw himself backward, trying to stay erect. The second bird struck. Coffin had one arm to protect his eyes. Somehow, blind in a moment that whirled, he drew his pistol and fired point blank.

The bird yelled. The softened slug had blown a hole entirely through the great body. One wing banged Coffin's head, before the creature fell. Its mate had released Svoboda and was circling about to make a fresh attack on him. Svoboda got his own gun free. He was too dizzy to aim straight, but he thumbed it to automatic fire and hosed the air with lead.

Two huge forms trailed blood down through the clouds.

Minutes afterward, Svoboda found strength to grab the rope, put his feet against the cliff, and climb back onto the ledge. The process was rough on Coffin, his anchor post, who was still only half conscious. Svoboda unclamped the other man's spike soles and stretched him out with his head pillowed on his pack. Coffin had a gash in his left cheek and a hand's-breadth bruise on his right temple. Svoboda was in better shape. His heavy jacket had warded off the bird's talons and his pack had absorbed the blow of its beak – though both were ripped. He felt numb with reaction.

When Coffin was awake, Svoboda gave him a stimpill and took half a tablet himself. Then they could talk. 'What in blazes was that?' Coffin asked feebly.

'A kind of spearfowl hitherto unknown,' Svoboda decided. He kept himself busy prying Coffin's spike soles loose from the ground and pushing the emergency blades

143

back into their slots against the phase-changing springplast. He didn't want to dwell on what had nearly happened. 'It's been observed that aerial life forms below the clouds tend to be much bigger than the corresponding upland species. More barometric pressure to support them, you see.'

'But I thought – the clouds were a boundary—'

'Yes, they are, as a rule. But evidently the giant spear-fowl will come this high once in a while. I'd guess they were after the air porpoises I noticed. That'd be a fat prey. I imagine we also looked tempting. Down at their own proper altitude, where their wings can really function efficiently, they must be used to hunting animals as large as us. Here, we could not have been lifted. But if we'd been knocked off and had fallen to the bottom, that'd serve the same purpose.'

Coffin covered his face. 'Oh, God,' he mumbled, 'it was like a monster out of Revelation. . . .'

'Don't worry about 'em. They're both disposed of, and I hardly expect there'll be any more. That particular species can't come this high very often, or in very large numbers, or they'd have been noticed by someone.' Svoboda refastened the soles to Coffin's boots. 'Think you can walk now? You didn't turn an ankle or anything?'

The older man climbed to his feet and tested his limbs gingerly. 'I'm okay. Battered, but nothing serious.'

'We'd better get started, then.' Svoboda moved to go around him.

'Hey!' Coffin barked. 'Where are you going?'

'Back. Where else? You surely don't plan to go on when—'

Coffin clamped fingers around Svoboda's wrist so hard that they left marks. 'No,' he said. It sounded like a stone falling.

'But for Anker's sake, man! Those birds – they must have been here yesterday, too – we *know* what happened to Danny.'

'We do not. If they had killed him, his bracelet would be intact.'

144

'Not if he got scared when he saw them, ran down the trail and fell. If the transmitter smashed on a rock —'

'If, if, if! We go on, I say!'

Svoboda stared into the fanatical eyes. Coffin stood unbending. Svoboda turned. 'Okay,' he said with hatred.

6

At the bottom of the promontory they were below the clouds, and the Cleft had merged with the general mountainscape. This continued its fall toward the coastal plains, but the trend of peaks and valleys, ridges and ravines, was not visible to a man afoot. For timberline merged with the clouds, in the form of gnarly little trees, and soon the forest enclosed him. He could gauge his rate of descent by an aneroid – or by the quickness with which the trees became tall, the temperature rose, and his head felt stuffy. From patches of meadow he could see alps, remote above the leaves, their highest points vanishing into the sky. He could note how swiftly the rivers ran and how deep their gorges were carved. But otherwise he knew only the forest.

If the boy had made it thus far, he would surely have lost his way in a few minutes. The searchers hung yet another beacon bracelet in a tree, checked compass and pedometer, and started off in a spiral. Not that they could maintain the pattern to more than the vaguest approximation, in that broken and overgrown country.

Eventually they must halt, for supper and sleep. Since, luckily, the weather didn't threaten rain, this involved little more than heating some food and inflating the sleeping bags. After placing a sentinel cell on a log to sweep the area with its beams, they lay down. Svoboda tumbled into unconsciousness.

A buzz awoke him. For a moment, disoriented, he thought it was the sentinel, then realized it was only his wrist-watch alarm. He didn't want to get up. However tired, he had slept badly. Muscles and head ached, his brain was clogged with half-remembered evil dreams. He unglued his eyes. Thirst made his mouth abominable.

'Here.' Coffin handed him a canteen. The older man was already dressed. His clothes were rumpled, his chin unshaven, the flesh seemed melted from his bones. But he moved with feverish energy and excitement tinged his voice. 'Hurry up and get functional. I've something to show you.'

Svoboda drank deeply, splashed water on his face, and crawled from the bag. His lungs toiled. According to the barometer, they were now at five Terrestrial atmospheres. Since carbon dioxide was denser than oxygen or nitrogen, it would have an even larger density gradient. He tried to control the hyperventilation it induced, but couldn't do much for the headache and mental fuzziness.

Clad, he went over to Coffin, who sat on the ground by a portable rack in which were several test tubes and a miniature electronic box with four dials. An ovoid yellow fruit, a cluster of red berries, a soft tuber, and a few varieties of nut were spread on the ground before him, together with some ampoules. Svoboda couldn't interpret his expression. Hope, eagerness, gratitude, awe?

'What've you got?' Svoboda asked.

'A food testing kit. Haven't you seen one before?'

'Not like that. I've seen Leigh drive around in his lab truck, checking plant and meat samples. Though not for a long time, come to think of it.'

Coffin nodded absently. His gaze was still on the apparatus. He spoke, lecturing on the obvious as well as the new, in such a quick harsh rattle that Svoboda realized he wasn't paying attention to his own words:

'No, you wouldn't have. Agrotechnic data on most species in the Emperor Valley were gotten by the first expedition. Leigh's work has extended further, into the deserts, the higher mountains, and the other continents, as well as studying what few lowland species have been brought back. With the cooperation of other specialists, he's worked out certain basic patterns. I'm surprised you haven't heard of his results, even if they aren't in your line of work. I know everybody's wrapped up in his own concerns, too busy developing his own specialty under alien conditions. But if we can't yet publish a scientific journal, don't you think we should hold periodic meetings?

'Well, in any event, Leigh's conclusions are very recent. You'd hear of them in time, because they're of interest to everyone. He has shown what could have been foreseen, that there is not an infinite range of dangerous compounds on Rustum. The same chemical series recur, just as the same starches and sugars and acids are found in Terrestrial plants. Theoretical studies have lately enabled him to predict beyond the data. For instance, he's found it's not possible that any native leaf can contain nicotine. It'd react with an enzyme known to be essential to Rustumite photosynthesis.

'On the foundation of such studies, Leigh's developed this portable testing kit. With high probability, any meat or vegetable sample which passes the battery here – simple color, precipitation, electronic and optical tests – anything which passes can be eaten by man. It'd probably lack certain vitamins and so on that we need, but it'd keep you alive for quite a while. He's given such kits to a number of farmers who're willing to experiment with domesticating native plants. Soon he will try to organize an expedition into the lowlands, to carry on an extensive program of tests. You and I happen to have anticipated him a bit in that respect.'

'You mean—' Svoboda's dulled understanding groped after significance. 'You mean you've been testing those things when you should have been sleeping?'

'I couldn't sleep much anyway. And I'd brought my kit along because ... for the same reason ... Leigh wants to promote that expedition. The highlands and lowlands are separate ecological zones. The few lowland species he's studied so far have given him hope that there may be many down here which are fit to eat. I'm beginning to think that must be true. These specimens here I gathered within a hundred meters of camp. All are safe.' The close-cropped bony head bowed low. 'Father,' Coffin murmured, 'I thank Thee.'

'You sure?' Svoboda asked, open-mouthed.

148

'I tried them myself, a couple of hours ago. Haven't gotten sick yet. They taste quite good, in fact.' Coffin smiled. It seemed to hurt his face, but was a smile nevertheless. 'Now, in autumn, the woods must be full of such fruit. I found poisonous ones too, of course, but they were obviously kin to highland forms we already know about. You can see that from the leaves alone.'

'Jumping Judas!' Svoboda's knees gave way. He sat down on the grass. 'You tried it yourself —'

An odd serenity grew in the other man. 'On the basis of the tests, the chance of these things being safe is good. But the final test was to eat them. If it's God's will that we find Danny alive, they are indeed safe.'

'But ... if you keel over ... I can't pack you out. You'll die!'

Coffin ignored the protest. 'You get my idea, don't you?' he said earnestly. 'By the time he got this far, Danny must have been ravenous. He's so small, too. He'd forget the prohibition and pluck something from a tree. But I think ... I trust ... God would strengthen his common sense, so he'd leave those fruits alone that he could tell by their appearance must be poisonous. Instead, he'd eat things like these before me.

'If I don't get sick, he hasn't. And – we needn't worry about food supplies, you and I. We can live off the country and continue the search for days.'

'Are you insane?' Svoboda breathed.

Coffin began to dismantle the apparatus. 'Why don't you make chow while I pack?' he asked mildly.

'Look here. Just a minute. You look here. I'll carry on till nightfall, since we do have proper stores for that long. But then we'll make camp for the dark hours —'

'Why? We have flashlights. We can also search by night, however slowly.'

'Because it'd be as fatal to break a leg in some animal burrow as it would be to trust ourselves to your neolithic God,' Svoboda exploded. 'Tomorrow at dawn I head back.'

Coffin reddened but suppressed a retort. 'Let's not argue

about that now,' he said after a moment. 'We may find him before sunset, you know. Come, do start some breakfast.'

They ate in silence. Trying to forget the ache in his head and muscles and to stop wearing himself out with tension, Svoboda looked at the woodland.

However oppressive the air, he could not deny that he saw majesty. They sat in a little meadow where a slow wind tossed the grass in bluish-green waves. Here and there stood dense bushes with berry clusters the color of rubies. The trees round about were tall and thick. One species resembled live oak – a trifle – the boles covered with what might on Earth have been called moss. Another was reminiscent of juniper, but the bark a deep red. A third was slim and white, crowned by leaves that were not solid but an intricate lacework. Between the trunks was underbrush, primitive plants whose leafage was a fringe along a thin flexible stalk. When wind or a foot passed through, a whispering rippled outward. Looking down high archways of branches, the human eye soon found darkness; but not unrelieved, for luminous fungi glimmered purple and gold out there.

The sky overhead was milky. It diffused radiation till you could not tell where the sun was, and no shadows were cast. Yet the light was ample: soothing, in fact, after years of the brilliance that bathed High America. A few weather clouds scudded beneath the permanent layer. (Which was not really permanent; there were often rifts, wonderfully blue.) The wind lulled in the trees.

If I could only stand the air! Svoboda thought.

If, as Coffin's findings suggested, indigenous lowland species actually were more beneficial than harmful to man, then man on Rustum was doubly tantalized. No doubt a settler here would have to supplement his diet with a few Terrestrial plants, but they need only be a few. Corn and potatoes, say, which ought to thrive under these conditions. For the rest, one might range freely over the planet.... But the damned atmosphere forbade it.

Svoboda stole a glance at Coffin. The other's long body

was more at ease than Svoboda remembered ever seeing; a raptness lay on the lantern-jawed countenance. No doubt he saw his discovery as a special dispensation, a chance to redeem his sin of letting Danny run away in the first place. *How long will he keep blundering around before he accepts that the boy is dead at the foot of that cliff? Till one or the other of us is dead, too? That won't take many Rustum days, in a chaos of unknown life forms, with our bodies poisoned by each breath we draw.*

I will not *stay down here with a lunatic.*

Svoboda touched the pistol at his side and looked toward Coffin's. *But will he let me go back?*

Resolution came. No need to provoke a quarrel yet, when twenty-odd hours of daylight remained. But tomorrow morning, or tonight if he insisted on proceeding in the dark, Coffin must somehow be disarmed and brought home at gun point.

I wonder if Teresa will thank me. Or forgive me.

Svoboda stubbed out his cigaret. 'Let's go,' he said.

7

The crisis came late in the afternoon.

They had lost all sense of time. Now and then they looked at their watches and noticed, in a dull far-off way, that the hands stood at a different angle. They took rest periods which became ever more frequent, but those were merely intervals of lying and staring upward. Once or twice they bolted some food and gulped some tea, hardly noticing it. Appetite had dwindled with the growth of physical wretchedness.

Narcosis, Coffin knew. His brain dragged the thought out word by word. *Too much carbon dioxide. Now there's starting to be too much nitrogen. The extra oxygen doesn't help appreciably. It's raw in the lungs.*

Thy will be done. But God's help was withdrawn. It had not been mercy when the fruit was found edible. It had looked that way at the time – that He who fed the children of Israel in the wilderness would not let Danny die – but as he fought through a wall of vines and staggered into a thornbush, Coffin understood that the food was a command. Since God had made it possible to search this kettle of hell in detail, His servant Joshua must do so.

No, I'm not that crazy. Am I? To think the Lord would remake a planet – or design it from the beginning, five billion years ago – to punish my one self.

I'm only trying to do my duty.

O Teresa, comfort me now! But her eyes and hands and voice were lost behind the clouds. There was only this forest, which fought him, and the breath that whined in his gullet. Only heat, and thirst, and pain, and thick alien smells, and a creeper that snared his feet so he crashed into a tree.

Somewhere a creature cawed, like laughing.

Coffin shook his head to clear it. That was a mistake.

The top of his skull seemed to tear off. He wondered if he dared swallow another aspirin. Better not. Save them.

It flashed in him: how queerly life worked out! Had it not been for that message sent after the fleet, he might be a spaceman yet. He might at this moment stand with Nils Kivi under a new sun, on a clean new world. Perhaps not, of course. Perhaps Earth had finally abandoned the star argosies, and the ships swung hollow about a planet that had ceased to breed men who wondered. But Coffin liked to think his old friends were still pursuing their trade. Vicarious pleasure, after a day breathing dust on a tractor.

To be sure, I would never have married Teresa.

Suddenly the commonplace observation, which he had made daily since he renounced his hopes, exploded. It struck him, so hard that he stopped and gasped, that she was not a consolation prize. If he could go back and undo those years, he wouldn't.

'What's the matter?' Svoboda croaked.

Coffin glanced back. The other face, dark-haired, hook-nosed, stubbly and sweaty and gaunt, seemed to waver in a fog of heat and silence, against a cosmos of blue-green leaves. 'Nothing,' he said.

'I think we'd better change course.' Svoboda gestured to the compass clipped on his belt. 'If we want to maintain the spiral.'

'Not immediately,' Coffin said.

'How come?'

Coffin didn't feel like explanations. He turned and lurched onward. He was too full of his own reassessment for speech.

But his body lacked strength to preserve the wonder. He began considering the immediate problem, how to bring Danny back for her. A lost and frightened boy would tend to follow the present sharp downgrade rather than go in a circle. Hence a straight line was a better search pattern than a spiral. Wasn't that so? One had to guess. God wouldn't condemn you for guessing wrong. Or anyhow, He might forgive you for Teresa's sake. The object of life was not to avoid a Jonathan Edwards hellfire, but to be upright and honorable.

Not that men ever achieved that object. Himself, Joshua Coffin, least of all. But he tried – sometimes. And he tried to teach his children the same ideal. They'd need it, not only for its own sake but as an added strength on this cruel planet. No, wrong; Rustum was not cruel. Rustum was simply big. And Teresa had said to him so often, honor wasn't enough. Survival wasn't enough. You had to be kind as well. Christ knew she had been kind to him, kinder than he deserved, kindest on those nights when the remembrance of his guilt came back. He had been too demanding, because he was afraid. The small grubby hands that plucked at his clothes were not a duty. Well, naturally they were, but duty and pleasure weren't necessarily separate. He'd always understood that. His duty as the captain of a ship had been his pleasure. But when it came to people, he had only understood it with the top of his mind. Which didn't count. He had to come down into this thick and silent forest before the knowledge really entered him. The Buddhists talked about living in the moment, unburdened by past or future. He had scorned it as an excuse for self-indulgence. But here, now, in some fashion he could see how difficult a way that was to travel. And was it so unlike the Christian's 'born again'?

His thoughts swirled into total confusion and were lost. Nothing remained but the tanglewood.

Until they emerged at the canyon.

Coffin had gotten so used to pushing through underbrush and climbing over logs that the sudden lack of resistance threw him to one knee. The pain jabbed tears from his eyes but called his mind back to lame life. Beside him, Svoboda drew a sharp breath, a sound quickly scattered by the wind that went booming under the sky.

Here the mountainside became so steep so fast that the slope was almost a cliff. The forest made a wall along its top. Down the sides, where the soil was eroded, there grew only grass and a few stunted trees. Boulders lay strewn

154

about and crags lifted weather-gnawed heads toward the rim. The opposite side was considerably lower, dim and blue to the eye, easily twenty kilometers away. The same vagueness of sheer distance blurred the ends of the gorge. Coffin had an impression it was stupendously long, whole mountains riven asunder, but could make out no details. He thought he glimpsed a river at the bottom, but of that he was also unsure. Too many pinnacles and bluffs, too much space, lay between.

He knew he should look on this masterwork of God with awe, but his head throbbed and his eyeballs felt ready to burst. He seated himself by Svoboda. Each movement was a separate task. His hands and feet were like chunks of lead.

Svoboda had struck a cigaret. The remaining rational part of Coffin thought, *I wish he wouldn't poison himself like that. He's too good a fellow.* The wind ruffled Svoboda's hair, as it did the leaves at their backs and the grasses beneath.

'Another Cleft,' the miner said inanely, 'at right angles to the one we know.'

'And we are the first of the human race to see it,' Coffin answered, wishing he were not too miserable to savor the fact.

Svoboda seemed equally blunted. 'Yeh. We've come further than the previous ground expedition, and the airborne trips to sea level never went in this direction. They have noted a lot such gashes elsewhere, though. Some tectonic process must cause them. A denser planet than Earth can hardly have identical geology. We certainly do get higher mountains here.'

'This isn't as sheer as the Cleft,' Coffin heard himself reply. 'The sides can retain soil, you notice. It's wider and longer, of course.'

'You'd expect that, where the topography is a bit less vertical.' Svoboda sucked smoke, coughed, and stubbed out the cigaret. 'Damn! I can't take tobacco any more, in this air. What're we mumbling about, anyhow?'

155

'Nothing important.' Coffin leaned against his pack. The wind blew the sweat out of his clothes so fast that he was soon chilled. The forest roared with wind. Its velocity was not great, but the pressure made it a near gale.

Windpower would be valuable when men were finally able to move down off the plateaux. When would that be? Not for many generations, surely. The mills of the gods grind slowly, but they grind exceedingly small. Not always slowly, though. The mills of change had ground faster than the dinosaurs could adapt to an altering climate, faster than science and technology could evolve to keep Earth's exploding population civilized. All Rustum was a millstone, turning and turning among the stars, and the seed of man was ground to powder, for it repented the Lord that He had made man. . . .

'Well,' said Svoboda, 'he'd scarcely have entered this ditch, so we'd better modify our search pattern.'

His words were such a welcome interruption, jarring Coffin from half-awake nightmare, that their meaning didn't penetrate at once. 'Eh?'

Svoboda scowled at him. 'By heaven, you look like a reclaimed corpse. I don't think you can even last out this day.'

Coffin struggled to sit up straight. 'Yes, yes. I'll get by,' he said thickly. 'What are you suggesting, though? About our course,' he added with care, to make sure Svoboda understood. Communication seemed intolerably difficult. *Sand in my synapses. I can't think any more. Neither can he. But I can keep going after my brains have quit. I'm not sure he can, or will.*

'I was about to propose we follow the verge of this canyon southward till dark, then tomorrow morning cut directly back toward the Cleft. That way we'll have described a large triangle.'

'But what if he went north? We have to work northward also.'

Svoboda shrugged. 'We can head north instead of south if you'd rather. It's a toss-up. But not both directions. We are not staying at this level past tomorrow. That's too big a risk. We haven't the right to take it. Not with families to support.'

'But Danny isn't dead,' Coffin pleaded. 'We can't abandon him.'

'Look,' said Svoboda. He sat cross-legged, ran a hand through his hair, gestured with an open palm. The horror was his trying to be reasonable, Coffin thought, and making nothing but empty noises. 'Let's assume the kid did not go off that cliff by the waterfall. Let's assume he reached the woods and did not eat something poison, or starve for fear of eating anything. Let's assume he did not drown in a pond, or get stung by one of the giant venom bees that've been seen in this country, or get attacked by some local equivalent of a catling. Those are damned big assumptions, too big for men to stake their lives on, but I'll grant them for the sake of argument. I'll assume he went blindly on in the forest, trying to find his way back but getting more and more lost, gradually slipping further and further down the mountainside. Well, then, do you realize how this air would weaken him? It's all I can do to move. After three or four days breathing this stuff, I wouldn't be fit for anything but to lie down and die. Danny's – he was – a child. Higher metabolism. Greater lung area relative to weight. Less muscular endurance.

'Coffin, he's dead.'

'No.'

Svoboda struck the ground with his fist till he had mastered himself. 'Have it your way.' The wind harried his words. 'I said I'd humor you – and Wolfe – to the extent of making that zigzag return tomorrow. That's the end, however. Savvy?'

'We could use a part of the night,' Coffin urged. 'Can you sit idle by a fire, thirty mortal hours, knowing Danny may be —'

'That's enough! Shut up before I belt you one!'

Coffin locked eyes with him. Svoboda's mouth grew taut. The last sense of his own righteousness drained from

Coffin. Nothing remained but regret, that he could not stop what must now happen. For a moment the sadness almost overrode his headache. He crawled to his feet. The wind pushed at his back, he must lean into it, the wind hooted and tried to push him southward along the canyon, which resounded with its noise. Svoboda still sat. *Forgive me. Judith was always good to Teresa. Forgive me, Jan.*

Coffin reached for his pistol.

'Oh, no, you don't!' Svoboda surged to his knees and threw himself forward. They went over together.

Svoboda's hand clamped on Coffin's gun arm. Coffin struck at him with his left fist. The younger man took the blow on the top of his head. Anguish lanced through Coffin's knuckles. Svoboda got his body across his opponent's stomach. His right shoulder jammed itself under Coffin's chin. He had him pinned, and both hands went to work, trying to pry the gun from the other man's fingers.

Coffin hit ribs and back with his half-crippled fist. Svoboda didn't seem to notice. Darkness whirled in Coffin's skull. *I am old, I am old.* He couldn't reach around the pack on Svoboda's shoulders, to help his right hand keep the pistol. Was it the wind that shouted in his ears, or was he about to faint?

His flailing arm struck something hard. Fingers closed on a knurled butt. Hardly knowing what he did, he pulled Svoboda's gun from its holster. He slapped the younger man's temple with the barrel. Svoboda cursed, let go Coffin's weapon and snatched after his own. Coffin hit him behind the ear with the freed pistol.

Svoboda sagged. Coffin was able to break his grasp and wriggle from beneath him. They lay close by each other, their faces buried in grass and soil. A leathery-winged animal flew low to investigate.

The guns in his hands brought Coffin alert first. He dragged himself beyond range of any sudden attack. Eventually he was able to stand again. By that time Svoboda was sitting up. The miner was white in the face. Blood matted his hair and trickled down his neck. He regarded

Coffin without speaking, for so long a time that the latter thought he must be seriously hurt.

'Are you all right?' Coffin whispered.

His words could not have crossed through the wind, but Svoboda must have understood. 'Yes. I think so. But you?'

'I wasn't hurt. Not to matter.' The pistols sagged. Svoboda began to rise. Coffin jerked both weapons back toward him. 'Don't move!'

'Have you gone out of your wits?' Svoboda rasped.

'No. I have to do this. I don't expect you'll ever pardon me. Take it to court when we get home. I'll pay any compensation I can. But don't you see, Danny has got to be found. And you'd end the search.' Exhausted, Coffin broke off.

'We never will get home this way,' Svoboda said. 'You've gone crazy. Recognize it. Give me those guns.'

'No.' Coffin couldn't take his eyes off the blood in Svoboda's hair. And the gray streaks. Svoboda was also aging. *We are one flesh, you and I,* Coffin wanted to say. *I know your fear and loneliness and weariness, your memory of being young and your puzzlement at youth being a memory, your dimming hope of one more hope before the inescapable moment. These are mine, too. Why have we hated each other?* But he couldn't say it.

'What do you want?' Svoboda asked. 'How long do we have to fumble about before you'll agree the boy is dead?'

'A few days,' Coffin begged. He wanted to weep, the tears stung his eyes, but he had forgotten how. 'I couldn't say for sure. We'll have to decide. Later.'

Svoboda watched him unmovingly. The thing with pterodactyl wings brayed at them: hurry up and die, will you? Finally Svoboda unhitched his canteen, washed himself and took a long drink.

'I may as well admit I was figuring to swipe your gun tomorrow,' he said. Wryness bent his lips upward.

'Must I tie you before I sleep?' Coffin groaned.

'Can you, even? I'm stronger than you. Put your weapons aside to tie me and see what happens.'

Grimness returned. 'There are ways to get around that,' Coffin said. 'You'll prepare slip knots under my direction, and put yourself into them. Now, march!'

Svoboda started south. Coffin followed at a safe distance. This direction was a slightly better bet than northward. Danny would have preferred the wind at the back, if he'd come this far. If that flying creature hadn't come directly from eating him. No! Such thoughts were forbidden.

It was easier to walk along the gorge than in the forest. Soon Coffin fell into the rhythm. His consciousness withdrew from pain and thirst and hunger and the mockery of the wind. He only needed his feet, his guns, one eye for the edge of the downslope and one for Svoboda. Dimly he noticed how often he stumbled, and how a slow darkening began to creep over the sky, but none of it was real. He himself wasn't real, he didn't exist, he never had, nothing existed but the search.

Until his radio-locator antenna swung about and pointed.

8

By the time they had slanted across ten kilometers of canyonside, they had fallen better than one more kilometer in altitude and were not far above sea level. The ache of body had almost disappeared in the blurring of mind. They slipped and staggered, fell, rolled over, reeled back to their feet and stared foolishly at blood where some rocks had cut their skin. Once Coffin asked, 'Is drunkenness like this?'

'Sort of,' answered Svoboda. He tried to steady the horizon. But the horizon was above him, a wall, its ramparts luminous, the lower courses black with approaching night. How idiotic to be underneath the horizon.

'Why does anybody get drunk?' Coffin clutched his head, as if to keep it from flying off.

'I don't.' Svoboda heard his voice ring from wall to canyon wall, prophetic, a bell as big as the world. 'Not often ... jus' a glow on —' Nausea seized him. He went on his knees. Coffin held him while he retched. They continued.

In the end they came to a crag which jutted out of the grass, straight into the wind, thirty meters of gray stone like some heathen monolith. High above, where the evening light caught its wings and made them shine, a giant spearfowl hovered. As the men went past the rock, the locator antenna swiveled backward.

Coffin stopped. 'Can you read uh dial?' he asked. 'M' eyes uh blurred.'

Svoboda squinted close. It was as if he saw the intensity meter through running water. Each time he tried to see where the needle was, it rippled. Sometimes the dial was close, infinitely close, a white planet with Mystery written on its face. Then it receded to infinite distances. A fever hum came out of it and filled the universe, whose walls crumbled, letting the galaxies spill forth into nothingness.

Svoboda persisted. He lay in wait, cat at a mousehole.

Eventually as he had foreseen, the meter stopped rippling for a second. He pounced. The reading was at maximum. Danny was here.

Svoboda ran around the pinnacle, calling. The base had a circumference of about seventy meters, buried in talus heaps. When he found Coffin again, he could only sit down, gasp, and point toward the top.

'He's up there?' Coffin repeated the question stupidly for a long while. 'He's up there? He's up there?'

Svoboda got out some stimpills. They had already taken so many that their hearts made their ribs tremble. These last nearly tore them apart. But their heads cleared somewhat. They could talk coherently, even think a little. They shouted and fired their guns. Nothing responded except the wind. The spearfowl made circles in heaven.

Coffin raised his binoculars. After a minute, wordless, he handed them to Svoboda and stood slump-backed. They brought the top of the spire close, and served as night glasses in this failing light. A litter of twigs, grass, and boughs extended over the upper edge.

'A nest,' Svoboda said. Horror touched him and would not let go.

'Must belong to that bird yonder,' said Coffin in a drained voice. 'We must have scared the bird off as we approached.'

'Well —'

Svoboda couldn't go on. Coffin astonished him by speaking it: 'The bird got Danny, or found him dead somewhere in this area. His bones are in that nest.'

His face was a blur in the gloom, but Svoboda saw the hand he extended. 'Jan,' he said, his tone begun to crack, 'I'm sorry I pulled a gun on you. I'm sorry for everything.'

'That's okay.' Svoboda took the hand. They didn't release each other for a while.

'Well,' said Coffin finally, 'we can't do more. Perhaps when O'Malley gets back from Iskandria he can take an aircar and see if there's anything left for burial.'

'I'm afraid there won't be, if the big spearfowl clean out

their nests periodically the way the highland species does.'

'No matter. Not really. For Teresa's sake, I wish we could have buried him. But God will still raise him up on the last day.' There was no comfort in the words. Coffin turned. 'We'd better see if we can get to the canyon brink before dark. We mustn't stay long at this altitude. I'm getting intoxicated again.'

Svoboda saw how he stooped and stumbled, and never understood what made him say, 'No, wait.'

'Eh?' Coffin asked like an old man.

'We've come this far. Let's not leave the job unfinished. This rock should be climbable.'

Coffin shook his head. 'I can't. I'm not able. I can hardly keep my feet.'

Svoboda dumped his pack on the ground and squatted beside it. 'I'll go,' he said. 'I am younger – have a smidgin of energy left. I can get there and back in half an hour or less. That still leaves time for us to reach the canyon top before it's quite dark at that level. Those clouds diffuse sunlight so much that dusk lasts for hours.'

'No, Jan. You mustn't. Judith —'

'Where's that obscenity rope?'

'Jan, wait till tomorrow, at least.' Coffin seized him by the shoulders. 'We'll come back here tomorrow.'

'I told you, by tomorrow there may be nothing left. We'd never know for sure. Here, strap this flashlight on my wrist. Where are those soles?'

Svoboda had mounted several meters before he really started wondering why. Surely this made no sense! In the deepening twilight he could scarcely see the roughnesses over which he climbed, except where the flashbeam fell. Descent would be easy enough: he'd drive an explosive piton, hang a rope from it, and slide. He could even lower a bundle of that which lay in the nest. But the ascent was dangerous. He hadn't seen from below just how eroded the crag was. Uneven, it offered foot- and hand-holds everywhere – but rotten rock, that kept breaking under his fingers. This was the only possible face to climb, in fact.

Everywhere else, whole sections had crumbled and fallen, to make shard piles at the base and leave scars up which a moonfly could hardly go. If a few tons of stone loosened under his weight, ten or twenty meters aloft, that was the end of Jan Svoboda.

Why? To recover some bones? They didn't need him. Judith and the children did. *His* children, not someone else's foundling.

A knob came loose in his hand. He released it and heard it go bouncing down. Blackness lay under his boots. While he crept higher, night had gulped the bottom of the crag, drowned Coffin, submerged the grasses and boulders; now it rose swiftly toward him. Was the top of the rock already in darkness? Or was that due to the vertigo which began to seize him? He looked at the stone, centimeters from his nose. It rippled. His head buzzed. He kept climbing because it was easier to drag himself onward than to think.

Until he came to a freshly made break. For twice a man's height above him, the crag turned lighter in hue and vertical. There were only two or three meters to go beyond that, but the top might as well have been on Raksh. Svoboda had exactly two pitons. They wouldn't let him span the gap.

He clung to his place. A gust of wind hooted in his ear and yanked at him. Finally his nerves steadied enough that he could open his eyes. *I did my best*. The thought was such a liberation that he understood why Coffin had drawn a gun and why he himself, Jan Svoboda, would have done likewise had his own son been lost. But here was the end. He took a piton from his belt, chose a spot with care – he didn't want to start another rockslide – and pressed the button.

In this air, the detonation was a thunderclap. Except for his spikes, he would have fallen. He wrung the dizziness out of his brain and made the rope's end fast to the iron. A fireman's slide back to earth, a few minutes' rest, and then the long march toward a pressure so low that he dared sleep.

O God, how he could sleep! Thirty hours would hardly be a wink.

'Father —'

Svoboda jerked. *No*, he gibbered. *I can't be that far gone. I mustn't be. I didn't imagine it. I only imagined I imagined it.*

'Father! Father?'

Danny looked over the brim of the nest.

Against the violet sky, where nothing lived but the bird of prey, his face showed startlingly white. The flashbeam revealed him thin and scratched and filthy, one eye black, blood clotted under the nose, and only rags remained of his shirt. Yet Danny Coffin looked out and cried for his father.

Svoboda shouted.

Danny began to weep. He sought to crawl down. Svoboda forced him back with curses. 'Crazy damn idiot, can't you see that scar, you'd fall and break your stupid neck! What happened, in hell's name? How'd you get there?'

The crying spell didn't last long. Danny hadn't many tears left. When he began to speak, he soon stopped snuffling and hiccoughing. Toward the end, his parched little voice was more clear than Svoboda's, and the answers he gave made more sense than the questions he was asked.

He had ventured into the Cleft in the runaway mood the adults had guessed. It evaporated in the course of descending through the clouds. When he reached the waterfall, cold, wet, and hungry, with night coming on, he had been quite prepared to turn back and take his punishment. But the two spearfowl attacked him. He fled down the ledge. A providential combination of fog and wind and rapidly gathering darkness kept the birds from pursuing him, once he had dodged their first clumsy rushes. But he dared not return. They might be waiting for him at the head of the trail – or so he thought in his panic. He continued in the other direction, groping on hands and knees till he collapsed, waking and continuing, until after some fraction of eternity he emerged in the woods. Dawn found him completely lost and famished. Some fruits and berries which looked different from the poison kinds at home attracted him. When he didn't get ill from them, he resolved to live off that sort exclusively till his foster father came. But this meant that he must keep moving, looking for more. He slept in trees or thornbrakes, drank from streams.

The eventual difficulty of finding water drove him into this gorge, toward the river. A big animal with tusks had seen him and given chase. He scurried to this rock and went up. Yes, it had broken under his feet; he grabbed a crack in time to save himself. The slide had frightened away the animal but left him trapped. Exhausted, he went to sleep. He must have slept right through the shouting and shooting below. The nearby crack of the piton charge had woken him.

'No, Mr. Svoboda, my head don't hurt, 'cep' where I hit it. I'm awful thirsty, but I'm not sick or nothing. Please, can you get me down to my father?'

As if in a dream Svoboda remembered someone remarking, somewhere, sometime, that Danny appeared to have an unusual carbon-dioxide tolerance. He must have, to get this far. To survive for an Earthly week under such conditions. He'd made a perfectly natural initial mistake, but once in the forest, he had kept his head as well as any adult. Better than most. Yes, absolutely better, thought Svoboda in his own drugged stupor. Danny's brain had stayed clear.

Danny's luck had held, too. The spearfowl was absent when he climbed into its nest and fell asleep. It didn't return from hunting till the men were so close that it wasn't about to land without inspecting these strange new animals. If they left, or if it decided they were harmless, it would come down.

And kill the boy.

'Please, Mr. Svoboda! My father's waitin'! I know he is! Please, I'm so awful thirsty, can't you help me?'

Svoboda stood on a tiny jut of rock, clinging to his rope. For a moment he hefted the extra piton. If he could throw that up, to be driven into the stone with a line attached –

No. He couldn't make any such cast from here, where it was impossible to swing his arm properly. Still less could he throw the piton, or a lasso, or anything, from the ground. A crossbow or catapult? No, where would he find materials to make one in appreciably less time than it would take to hike back to the settlement for help? Useable cord didn't grow ready-made in the woods.

The spearfowl soared closer.

Defeat rose in Svoboda's throat like vomit. He told the knowledge over and over, a kind of litany to the malevolent God who had arranged matters in precisely this way. *Sure, I can lie in wait till the bird comes near enough to shoot. But what then? We still can't reach the kid. Even if we started straight back home and traveled the whole night without stopping – which is not physically possible – and brought an aircraft which the winds didn't smash against a mountainside – even if we did, it would take fifty hours or more. The kid's dehydrated already. Listen to that mummy voice.*

Which is best, to let the spearfowl get him, or to let him die of thirst?

'Please, please! I'm sorry I ran away. I won't do it any more. Where's my father?' Danny's words trailed off in a dry rattle. He slumped at the edge of the nest. The wind tossed his hair and the tatters of his shirt like wild flags.

Through the querning in his skull, Svoboda heard a scrabble below him. He heard Coffin call, 'Danny, Danny,' and thought crazily the name was Absalom. Coffin couldn't make it up. He hadn't the strength. Svoboda couldn't go further. Danny couldn't climb down. Only the spearfowl was able to move. Impatient, it was nearing the crag in long spirals at whose lowest point the beak and the steel-gray feathers could be seen and the whistling heard in its pinions. Even through the wind, Svoboda could hear that whistle.

It came to him what he must do. Perhaps there was a better answer, an easy means of rescue, but his brain was too fogged to discover it. Danny lay still. By now, with the flashbeam off him, he was a black hump on the blackly silhouetted crag. Svoboda's free hand closed on the gun Coffin had returned. The butt felt heavy even before he had drawn. A snap shot, one merciful bullet into that hump. No more would be needed. The search would be at an end. Svoboda could go down the rope.

The ground was completely black under his feet. 'Danny,' Coffin called once more. The rubble at the pinnacle base clattered as he slid back. 'Jan, what can we do?'

Svoboda snicked the safety catch free but didn't draw his gun yet. He faced the wind, hoping the poison smoke would be blown out of his head, but the wind scorned him with dust in his eyes. He heard the spearfowl swoop closer still. Once it cried, a clear bugling that echoed from rocks which the night had overflowed. When he looked, he saw the great wings were still high enough in the canyon that they shone.

Why should the spearfowl not have him? he thought wildly. *Why shouldn't it have us all? It belongs here, it's strong and beautiful, we're the monsters from outer space, trying to take its home away. Come on down, vulture-beaked God. I'll give him to you.*

An answer struck.

Svoboda stood where he was, in wind and darkness, turning the idea over. A thought was as heavy as a millstone. He turned it and turned it, until the noise was like wind and great wings beating, until the mill ground the ocean full of salt. When he spoke, it was as if someone else talked for him, a whisper amid whirling and grinding. 'Danny! Danny, can you hear me? Listen! Are you awake? I can get you down!'

The flashbeam picked the small pinched face out of the murk. Danny roused himself from the half faint of exhaustion and despair. 'Sure,' he mumbled. Then, more clearly: 'Gee, you're swell, sir. What've I got to do?'

'Listen. Both of you,' Svoboda called. 'Danny, you've got to be brave. You've been brave so far. One last time, sport. Play dead. That's what you do. Play dead and let the spear-fowl land beside you. Then grab its legs. Grab tight and hang on. Got me, Danny? Can you do that?' The millstone groaned and sundered. He thought the boy had answered, but wasn't sure. He couldn't even be certain that Coffin had understood it. He snapped off his light and clung where he was, death still.

Now the bird was too low for the radiance lingering on the heights to touch it. Against the deep purple of the sky, which they seemed to fill, the wings were as black an outline as the rock. He drew his pistol. Shadows hid him. He could scarcely see the weapon himself.

The bird called challenge. There was no response. Too late, Svoboda realized he should have explained his idea in more detail. No time now. The spearfowl landed on the side of the nest. The vast wings folded. It looked over Danny like a hunchbacked giant.

The boy sprang and caught it by the legs.

As the bird shrieked and took off, Svoboda fired. He was never conscious of having aimed. But the spearfowl screamed once again. Danny hung athwart the sky like a bell clapper in the wind. The bird's blood pumped over him.

A final time the spearfowl struggled to rise. It won so much distance that Svoboda saw light again on its wings. They threshed more weakly. The spearfowl sank, braking itself, going down into darkness to do battle with the monster.

Svoboda slid along the rope so fast he skinned his hands.

A gun barked twice. When Svoboda arrived, the spear-fowl was dead. Coffin threw pistol and flashlight aside. 'Danny,' he wept. 'Danny, son.' They fell into each other's arms.

9

Sunshine came through crisp white curtains, reflected off a bowl of water, and made waves on the opposite wall. A cool gust followed into the bedroom. Outside, the lawn was still green but the gimtrees had turned color, scarlet streaked with gold, and the Hercules Mountains were blue and dim through a haze not unlike Earth's Indian summer.

Judith opened the door for Theron Wolfe. Svoboda laid his book on the blanket. 'Well,' said the mayor, 'how are you today?'

'Fine,' grumbled Svoboda. 'I don't see why I have to stay here. Damn it, I've got work to do.'

'The doctor said strict bed rest till tomorrow,' Judith reminded him sternly. 'You can't laugh off a case of exhaustion.'

'If it consoles you any, Joshua's been ordered a full day more than you, and is being even meaner about it,' said Wolfe. He planted his large bottom on a chair and took a cigar from his shirt pocket.

'How's Danny?' Svoboda asked.

'Oh, he's quite recovered and having the time of his life,' Judith said. 'Teresa's kept me posted. If you'll excuse me, mayor, I must get back to work. We are positively going to have that wedding day after tomorrow, as soon as Josh can come.'

The door closed behind her. Wolfe pulled a flat bottle from beneath his jacket. 'Aged in the wood,' he whispered hoarsely. 'My best run so far.'

Svoboda took the present without feeling unduly grateful. 'I trust you came to make some explanations,' he said.

'Ahem! If you wish. Not that I see what there is to explain. You and Josh brought the kid back. So you're both heroes. And, while it's none of my business, I think Josh solved a few personal difficulties in the course of the trip.

I've never seen him look honestly happy before today.'
Wolfe lit the cigar and puffed ostentatiously before adding:
'To be sure, you'll be interested in the medical report on
Danny.'

'Huh?' Svoboda sat straight. 'You said he was okay.'

'Yes, yes. But he got a thorough checkup, and it turns out
his tolerance to high air-pressures is more than usual. It's
fantastic. Oh, none of this mutant superman nonsense. He
simply lies at one extreme end of the normal distribution
curve. But he can live quite comfortably at sea level if he
chooses. I suppose,' Wolfe continued thoughtfully, 'that's
why he was always inclined to build bright daydreams
about the world below the clouds. He never associated
descent with discomfort, even to the subliminal degree that
you and I do in the course of walking downhill on this
plateau. He must have noticed that other children did get
cranky when they had gone too far down the northern slope
of the tableland. So, since they made him an outcast, his
imagination looked toward the place they couldn't enter.'

Svoboda took a pull at the bottle and passed it over. 'I
wish something could be done about the way that kid is
teased. He's got too much guts and intelligence to rate it.'

'Oh, that's no longer a problem,' Wolfe answered. 'Since
he played Robinson Crusoe where nobody else could have
survived, Teresa says his schoolmates hang on his every
word. Furthermore, I intend to publicize his true importance. He's the most important human being on Rustum.
Let's hope it doesn't go to his head.'

'How come?'

'Use your own head, man. Danny's the first real Rustumite. When he's grown, he can go anywhere and do anything
on the whole damn planet. His descendants will out-
number everybody else's, by virtue of being so much better
fitted to survive. I hope and expect that among the other
exogenes there'll be some more like him. The sperm and
ova donors were chosen with such a possibility in mind.
But even if nobody in this generation quite matches Danny,
he can take the lead. Long before High America gets too

171

crowded, there'll be people pioneering the lowlands. They'll keep the spirit of liberty alive on behalf of everyone else.'

Slowly, Svoboda nodded. 'I see. Should have thought of that myself, if there hadn't been so much distraction.'

Wolfe clapped him on the arm. 'And you, Jan, saved this priceless treasure for us,' he declaimed. 'Even if the simple fact of your heroism were not sufficient, which it is, the value of your service to the future is going to make you the most admired figure on the planet. Write your own ticket, boy. Would you like to be the next mayor? Would you like a hundred skilled workers to start a new mine for you? Name it and it's yours. So aren't you glad I pushed you?'

Svoboda shook the hand loose. Anger clouded his face. 'Come off that,' he said.

'Why, Jan.' Wolfe raised his brows. 'Aren't you pleased?'

'Well ... I'm glad the boy was saved and so forth. I'm even glad I went myself. It's something to remember. But I don't want any stupid publicity.'

'You've got it. Willy-nilly, you've got it.' Wolfe laid his finger along his nose. 'Can't be helped. All High America knows of your deed. Hasn't Judith told you how many 'phone calls she's gotten? The flowers and deputations will start arriving as soon as you're on your feet.'

'Look here!' Svoboda rapped. 'I know you, Theron. You're a nice, intelligent, obliging, cheerful, free-wheeling son of a bitch. You didn't know about Danny's chromosomes when you blackmailed me into going after him. All you knew was, Josh and I were valuable citizens in a severe labor-shortage economy; and Danny was one small boy, with plenty more where he came from. Why did you send me down there?'

'Well, now.' Wolfe stroked his beard. 'Ordinary altruism. Human decency. I'd have gone myself, were I not so old and fat.'

Svoboda said a nasty word. 'The devil you would,' he added. 'You had some other purpose in mind. Okay, you've led the colony better than anyone else would have, I suppose. We haven't needed a pleasant little humanitarian to

172

guide us; we needed exactly the kind of ruthless bastard you are. So Josh and I were your pawns. Okay. But I demand to know why.'

Wolfe studied his cigar ash. 'You probably do have the right,' he said. 'And I can trust you to keep a secret. Trouble is, my reasoning's rather hard to explain. I feel it, sharp and hard as a knife. But the words are fuzzy.'

Svoboda settled back. 'I'm waiting,' he said.

Wolfe chuckled. He crossed one leg over the other and blew a plume of smoke. 'Well,' he said, 'remember that Josh's neighbors would only help him scout the plateau, where they were safe. To a man, they refused to enter the Cleft, though Danny had obviously gone in that direction. They pleaded harvest time. That is, their precious crops were more important than that boy's life.'

'Uh —' Svoboda blushed. 'Uh.... If the crops had been spoiled by a rainstorm, the whole community would've had a lean year.'

'That's a crappy argument. So what? No one would have starved. We'd have tightened our belts for a Rustumite year, eight or nine Terrestrial months. Do you seriously mean you'd have let a child die, alone, possibly in great pain, so you could have an extra serving on your plate for the next eight months?'

'N-n-no. If you put it like that. Nobody did, however. I myself ... I mean, the likelihood of success wasn't in proportion to the hazard.'

'Again, so what? In early times on Earth, a hundred men would have been honored to risk their necks on the off chance that one life could be saved. You'd have gone after a child of your own, wouldn't you? No tepid calculation of probabilities in that case, eh? So did Danny have less claim on you because he wasn't your personal flesh and blood?

'What did we come to Rustum for? To live our own lives as we see fit, without official nosiness. Good enough. But we've carried it too far. Now that the initial struggle to survive is past, each family has retreated more and more into its own selfish concerns. We can't have that. Man can't live alone. The lost, and sick, and weak, and poor have got to be helped, or how can we depend on their help when our own luck runs out? If we won't voluntarily do this, then in the end, inevitably, there will be laws and police to make us do so. A community can't exist without public service.

'I want to curb that tendency on Rustum. The more citizens who perform public duties of their own free will, out of a sense of responsibility, the less government and the fewer coercive laws we'll need. Nor will we get so slack and indifferent that laws can be tied onto us when we aren't looking. We need a tradition of mutual help. Our heroes have got to be not the men who gained the most, but those who gave the most.'

Wolfe broke off, red-faced. 'Pardon me,' he finished. 'I didn't mean to preach. We need a workable psycho-dynamic symbology. Words are too imprecise. What starts out to be a sociological observation turns into a sermon.'

Svoboda grinned. 'You're a frustrated do-gooder your-self, Theron. Go on.'

'Not much else to say,' Wolfe answered. 'I'd been watching for an opportunity like this. Now you've set an example. By unmerited good fortune, your attempt succeeded spectacularly, which underlines the lesson in red. I shall make sure that everybody has their noses rubbed in it. This is going to be one community most powerfully ashamed of itself. I'll use the mood to talk more people into setting still more examples. Maybe in a few years the seed we've planted will start to grow.'

He lumbered to his feet. 'I'm sorry you had to be the goat, though, Jan.'

'I'm not.' Svoboda grimaced. 'Except – Judas priest! – do you mean I have to pose as some bloody kind of shining knight?'

' 'Fraid so. That's the real service you can render us. And the hardest.' Wolfe chuckled. 'Courage. Whatever the world may think of you, remember, in your most inmost soul you're rotten.'

174

Svoboda laughed with him. Wolfe bade adieu. Svoboda didn't return to his book at once. He lay for a while gazing out the window, toward the horizon where the snowpeaks of Hercules upheld the sky.